# THE PAINTING
## OF THE
# WHITE WOLF

Carlos Alberto Garabelli

THE PAINTING OF THE WHITE WOLF

The characters and events depicted in this story are entirely fictional. Any resemblance to real persons (living or dead) or actual events is purely coincidental.

ISBN: 979-8-3327-5993-2

Book design by Sarah E. Holroyd (https://sleepingcatbooks.com)
Cover design by Natalia Llamas

With gratitude, I acknowledge my lovely wife Maria Luisa for her steadfast support and thoughtful reactions to the manuscript, as well as my dear friend Loraine Cook for her outstanding help in proofreading the English version.

# I

## Richmond, Virginia, February 2006

IN THE WINDOW OF the third-floor tenant, the snow continues to accumulate against the ledge. Below, an old lamppost dimly lights the alley, revealing the speed of the flakes that are already settling on the roofs of the cars. The pillars of the highway that flies over the side of the building shelter a couple of homeless men, standing around a fire in a metal barrel. The flames cast fleeting strokes of light on their faces as they warm their hands. Inside the bedroom, the furniture stands as blurry shapes, like statues in the dimness. Only the bathroom light remains on. The door, barely ajar, releases a beam of incandescent light that stretches long across the floor. As it travels, it fades into mid-tones on the parquet, conforms to the relief of the baseboard, and stretches again in a toasted strip along the wall until it meets the ceiling. Adrián Fontana lies face down with his right arm under the pillow. The left one hangs off the side of the bed. He exhales from his powerful lungs a grizzly bear's snore that assaults the silence of the early morning. His breath, a heady mix of whiskey, beer, and cognac, has enough intensity to intoxicate the air near the bed. The gust of his breath stirs the ashes of the crushed cigarette butts in the ashtray. The sudden sound of a bell disrupts the rhythm of his snorts. His eyelids twitch slightly. It sounds distant, like in another room. He turns his head to the opposite side of the pillow. The ringing sounds closer. He blinks, hesitant, still numbed by the drunkenness. The ringing now screeches almost next to his bed. Annoyed, he lets out a snort. He realizes it's the phone. He turns on the lamp and stretches his arm, making clumsy and uncoordinated swipes towards the receiver. He accidentally knocks over a picture frame on the nightstand, which falls to the floor. He curses and puts it back on the table. He picks up the receiver and, through gritted teeth, mutters a gruff "hello" to whoever is the idiot disturbing the truce his body requires. He had been drinking until midnight at Kuba-Kuba, his favorite joint. He goes there every night after dinner to avoid lingering with his ghosts. The pub is a block from his apartment. He sits at the bar, sometimes alone and sometimes with his occasional conquests. He spends a long time not listening to them, nodding automatically. But he remains absorbed in his thoughts.

On the other end of the line, a slightly choked voice says: "Hello, Adrián." He hesitates for a second. He knows that voice. It's Sofía, the one in the picture frame on his nightstand. "Sofía?"

"Yes. Sorry about the hour, but I need to talk to you."

"Are you okay?"

"I need your help," says the woman he was about to marry. The only one who had awakened in the cynical labyrinths of his mind the desire to share a lifetime together.

"Can we meet at your office in an hour, please?" she continues. "I still have the key. If I get there first, I'll wait inside."

He says yes without hesitation. He'll be there at 6:30. He hangs up and leaves the bed with robotic clumsiness towards the shower. He mutters an angry "Fuck!" as he crashes his big toe against the shower door. He chooses to barely open the hot water faucet to receive the icy slap that will wake up his muscles and get his blood circulating. Why is she calling after so long? He dries off halfway and dresses in the same wrinkled clothes he left on the chair in the bedroom. He grabs his coat and hat from the hanger by the door. He descends the stairs two at a time, the iron steps creaking under his 180 pounds and 6-foot height. It's still snowing. The sub-zero Richmond cold hits his face.

"Start, damn it!" he orders after turning the ignition key of the '69 Ford Mustang he bought at a collector's auction. The machine roars to life. While the engine warms up, he clears the snow from the windshield with his hands. Without time or patience to finish the job, he gets back inside, shifts into first gear, and accelerates hard. The eight cylinders roar in the silent neighborhood. The Mustang slips on the first twenty meters of black ice, spewing a dense trail of white smoke that hangs in the frozen air. Adrián Fontana races along Route 195 towards Shockoe Bottom, the historic center of the city. Almost nothing impresses or startles him anymore. His profession and the personal disasters of his worn-out thirty-eight years have taken care of numbing his sensitivity. However, Sofía's call is the exception to the rule. He hasn't heard her voice in the three years since their final separation, even though she stubbornly and frequently infiltrates his nightmares or watches him from the empty chair at dinner. What does she want now? He doesn't entertain the possibility that she's going to forgive him. It must be something else. Is she in danger? The anxiety these questions cause him makes him press harder on the accelerator. The tires pierce the stillness of Shockoe Bottom, screeching under the brake's grip. It's 6:20. Ten minutes before the appointment. He is not known for his punctuality, but it's Sofía, and she still awakens his best intentions of civilized behavior. His office is on the fifth floor of an old Victorian building constructed in the late nineteenth century. It has an elevator with sliding iron doors, the kind that lets you see the stairs and the entrances to the offices as you ascend. He steps out of the grated box and sees the light escaping through the transom above the door. Sofía is already there.

"Crooked like the owner!" he grumbles before entering, while straightening the sign on the door that reads: Adrián Fontana-Private Detective.

# II

A BANKER'S LAMP WITH its characteristic emerald-colored glass barely illuminated the contours of the desk. To the right, near the phone, stood the same photo frame of Sofía that the detective kept on his nightstand. A half-open drawer revealed a jumble of photographs and the tool of his trade: a Nikon camera with a telescopic lens.

The rest of the room was almost in darkness, conveniently hiding the mess, dust, and cobwebs clinging to the bricks and ceiling. Papers were scattered everywhere on the desk, on the floor, overflowing from the wastebasket. The ashtray was piled high with cigarette butts. The Venetian blind had a few broken slats and hung askew, raised only halfway. Next to the entrance door was a marble table with a poorly washed coffee pot and empty sugar packets scattered around a cup decorated with the Uruguayan flag. The open bathroom door revealed a tiny, narrow room where one had to squeeze sideways between the sink and the wall to reach the toilet, almost pressing the stomach against the sink.

Sofía was facing away from the door, leaning on the desk with her head in her arms. When she saw him enter, she turned and glanced at him sideways but did not stand up. She straightened in the chair. He felt strange, almost uncomfortable. He had wanted to embrace her but no longer felt he had the right. He moved behind her and sat in the swivel chair. Her eyes were swollen, and her makeup was smeared. However, she looked at him with pupils as cold as Richmond's chill. After three years, he was again facing the woman from the photo frame on his nightstand, the one he caressed every night before going to sleep. The kisses, the passionate sighs, the jokes, and her girlish, tickling laughter were all in the past, mercilessly dissipated by time, which now returned her to his office with her youth shattered. She was still an attractive woman, with curly hair, harmoniously arched eyebrows, and a gypsy's full lips that had always captivated him. But her eyes no longer reflected her soul. They had turned a dark amber, like buckwheat honey. He did not know the reason for her distress, but he was painfully aware that the first time he had seen the pain and disillusionment reflected in her face, he had been the cause.

He stretched his arm across the desk, placed his imposing fingers on his ex-girlfriend's pale hand, and asked calmly, "What happened, Sofía?"

"They found my sister dead," she said, stiff and unyielding. "Strangled."

Adrián blinked and barely parted his lips. He was struck by the way she said it, almost with the professional coldness of a prosecutor or a forensic doctor.

"Look, read this," she said, handing him the digital version of a newspaper she took from her purse. The front page of El Observador announced in huge letters the murder of Carlota Ferraro, the daughter of Donato Ferraro, the deceased magnate of the food industry. The body had been found by the doorman after the building's neighbors noticed a nauseating smell coming from the victim's penthouse. The reading chilled him to the bone. Sofía's older sister, who had moved through life as if immortal, once untouchable, overwhelming in personality and power, was now reduced to another statistic of a brutal crime, like the many that had started to shake Montevideo in the 1990s, after he and Sofía had emigrated to the United States. She to finish her master's in law; he, to pursue his dream of a career in criminology.

Adrián looked away from the newspaper and searched her eyes. She held his compassionate gaze without blinking; for a moment, she gave herself a respite and lowered her head. She looked up again, serious, resolved, with almost vertical eyebrows, a hard mouth, and her chin tilted towards her neck. Then she asked him to travel to Montevideo to investigate the crime. She explained that she had discussed it with Anthony and that they would cover all the accommodation expenses and pay him thirty thousand dollars to find the culprit. Anthony was the happy bearer of the detective's shattered dreams. He had married Sofía after their breakup. Adrián's stomach churned at Anthony's neat and responsible attitude towards life, qualities that Sofía admired and which he lacked. Sofía had met Anthony at university, and they had graduated in the same year, both Summa cum laude.

They had started working at the law firm of the young man's father, a third-generation lawyer who had a prestigious law firm in downtown Richmond.

"I appreciate the confidence, but surely there are more experienced investigators in Montevideo to find the culprit," said Adrián as he stretched to empty the ashtray into the wastebasket.

"Please, don't give me that! We both know you can't trust the police," Sofía replied, irritated.

He knew she was right, but given Carlota's history, he did not want to be the one to bring to light the sordid secrets of a twisted life in front of Sofía. He knew the victim had been involved with military men from the dictatorship era. Perhaps they were the ones behind the murder.

"Sofía, I don't know if it's a good idea for me to get involved. Particularly, given my close relationship with your family. I could contact my friend, "Rabbit" Vergara. He knows many influential military men."

"No military men! They're all corrupt!"

"But it's just that . . ."

"Don't worry, I'll face whatever you discover," she interrupted, making it clear she had read his thoughts. "At this point in my life, I'm seasoned with surprises."

The detective caught the irony. He lowered his head, took out a cigarette, and put it to his lips without lighting it. He got up, walked to the window, and stood with his back looking into the void. Then he lit the cigarette.

"At least my father didn't live to see what happened to his favorite," she said.

"Why me, Sofía?"

"You're the only detective I know who speaks Spanish and, on top of that, is Uruguayan."

She got up, walked to the window, grabbed his arms, and added, "You owe me, Adrián!"

The detective wanted to keep refusing, but he couldn't fight the justice her eyes demanded. The call of blood that did not negotiate distances.

She returned to the chair and grabbed her purse. They agreed to keep in touch by phone and said goodbye.

Adrián sank back into his cracked leather chair, his gaze fixed on the photo frame. He stretched out and wiped the dust off with his coat sleeve. Then he turned off the lamp, leaned back, and stayed thinking in the dark until sleep overcame him.

# III

## Montevideo, mid-March 2006

THE WHEELS OF THE Boeing 747 bounced twice and continued their wild run down the runway of Montevideo Airport, prompting applause from the passengers for the delicate landing maneuver in the windy skies of the eastern pampas. Adrián Fontana had not returned to Uruguay since his mother's passing. The elderly woman was the only thing that motivated him to return to the southern seas. Now that she was gone, only reminiscences of Sofía remained, and he had no masochistic intentions of reliving the memory of a romance that had begun there, in the cobblestone streets of the old city, at the port market, on walks along the Pocitos promenade, and at the cinemas on 18 de Julio Avenue.

It was three in the afternoon. The sticky heat of the last vestiges of summer hit him in the face as he left the terminal. In the parking lot, the rental car awaited him, a Honda Civic with a manual transmission, like most cars that drove on national territory. Used to driving automatic transmissions in the United States, returning to press a clutch to shift gears was a source of joy, like a child reuniting with a forgotten toy. He headed down Rafael Barradas Street to the Carrasco coastal road towards the Hermitage Hotel, the same one from his last visit.

"The most beautiful promenade in the world!" he murmured, entranced, repeating the same phrase as every return. On the right flank, the imposing Carrasco Hotel Casino battled against time, waiting for a renovation that never came. He shortened the distance by taking the shortcut on Coimbra Street, and at the end of the slope, he admired the privileged location of the chalets lined up towards the Punta Gorda beach. In the distance, on the shore, two fishermen newly arrived from the sea in a red skiff were untangling corvinas from the nets to sell to the first buyers approaching. He remembered when he used to buy fresh fish there, the only one his mother would accept in the kitchen without hesitation.

He gently caressed the accelerator, enjoying the snake-like turns of the seaside drive. He was not in a hurry. He delighted in the landscape until he saw the hills of the Buceo cemetery descending towards the promenade. He glanced at them sideways, as if with annoyance. According to what they said, his father was buried there. He clenched his teeth and pressed the accelerator pedal to the floor just as he entered the curve of death, the tomb of countless teenagers who had succumbed behind the wheel, drunk with alcohol and adrenaline. The Honda's tires screeched hysterically on the sharpest angle of the asphalt, where the white and Moorish bulk of the Oceanographic Museum stood, with its solitary and narrow tower stretching towards the sky like a pointed pencil.

At the beginning of the century, a morgue had operated there, a humid and gloomy place where bodies arrived to be examined before being buried in the Buceo cemetery. After it was closed, the premises were abandoned for a few years, and rumors spread that diabolic spirits had taken residence there. In 1925, an

Italian set up a luxurious cabaret for the local aristocracy. A decade later, due to a crime that occurred in
the nightclub's basement, along with another story of
a woman who had climbed up the tower and jumped
into the void, it was dubbed, like the road that surrounded it: The Cabaret of Death. The locals attributed
the unsolved crime and the woman's suicide to the
spirits of the old morgue.

Adrián was not superstitious, but he had always
been attracted to these stories, and every time he
passed by, his eyes would wander to the facade. After
exiting the curve, he slowed down and continued driving at a cruising speed. The waves of the river as wide
as the sea rocked the schooners of the Buceo port, and
the smell of saltwater wafted through the car window.
Ahead, the skyscrapers of Pocitos beach stood tall.
Everything was just as it always had been. Unlike in
the United States, where the urban landscape under-
went rapid changes, time had stood still in Montevideo. The detective loved this geographical divergence
and crossed his fingers that it would always remain so.

The Hermitage Hotel was located two blocks from
the coast. Two years earlier, it had seemed ideal for
walking to the beach and scattering his mother's ashes

in the waters of the Río de la Plata. Now, the hotel's location once again proved strategic. It was three blocks from Carlota Ferraro's penthouse.

"Welcome, Mr. Fontana, long time no see!" exclaimed the reception manager with an effusive smile, extending his hand. He wore a noticeable toupee that Adrián always tried not to look at.

"How are you, Manuel? Do you still remember me?"

"I never forget a face or a name, and apparently, neither do you. Pleasure or business trip?"

"Neither" replied the detective, while glancing at a young receptionist who had already fixed her eyes on him. They chatted for a few minutes about the last World Cup, the exhausting heat, and the long journey.

"Graciela, the keys to room 503 for Mr. Fontana, please," ordered the man with the shiny wig. The young woman looked away from the newcomer, turned around, and stretched to the third key slot. Adrián took advantage of the maneuver to admire the suggestive roundness of her backside.

He went up to his room on the fifth floor. It faced Benito Blanco Avenue, where Pocitos almost ends, and Punta Carretas begins, with its old mansions and loose-tiled sidewalks that incited the outraged curses of men when, on rainy days, they splashed water and mud into their pants, or the subtle and more modest protests of society ladies when their high heels broke.

He checked his watch. It was five in the afternoon. He decided to take a nap to recover from jet lag. At seven, he woke up, took a shower, and went for a walk in the neighborhood. The fluorescent colors of the bar signs reminded him of his last trip through Spain and the Italian boot. They had the genetic signature of the origin of Uruguayans stamped on the facade. He stopped at the kiosk on Avenida Brasil, bought cigarettes, and a bottle of whiskey. He returned to the hotel and ordered a canned beer, two portions of anchovy pizza, and one of fainá to be brought to his room. That night he did not feel like eating out.

After dinner, he turned on the television and channel-surfed with the remote, entertained by the local flavor of the shows, with the unique idiosyncrasies of Uruguay and Argentina, so different from the rest of Latin America or the United States. After a while, he lost interest. He looked at the clock. It was ten o'clock at night. The same feeling of loneliness and emptiness that he had been experiencing for the past thirty-six months overwhelmed him. He morbidly marked in his mental calendar the time that had passed since he had lost the joy of living. Only the usual ritual remained. Before going to sleep, he took the picture frame out of his suitcase and placed it on the bedside table. He opened the bottle of Johnny Walker. He lay back on the bed with the glass full of what he sarcastically called his medicine. The one that numbed the memory of Sofía. After a while, the excesses, the sins, the twisted ghosts of the past slowly quieted down. He closed his eyes, defeated by the alcohol, and fell asleep, lying on his back, with the glass in his hand, resting on the sheets.

# IV

To an American tourist waking up in the Pocitos neighborhood, the invasion of high and varied decibels entering through the window in the early morning hours would certainly be surprising. The overwhelming and impertinent car horns, motorcycles with open exhausts, or the pneumatic hammers of workers breaking concrete as soon as the sun rises would irritate the nerves of even the calmest of Northern blondes. Despite having lived for a long time in the Richmond neighborhoods, where not even a fly was heard, the noise of the city did not disturb Adrián. He still had the first twenty-seven years of his life in Montevideo etched into the hard drive of his memory.

The bustle served to wake him up without having to set the alarm clock. He took a cold shower to revive his blood. After drying off, he splashed a generous amount of Agua Brava over his hair and rubbed it on his face as well. This gave him a feeling of well-being and freshness to which he had become addicted since the first time Sofía gave him what became his favorite cologne. He chose a white guayabera shirt, cargo pants, and a Caribbean hat, all in sober colors to avoid drawing attention. He knew that the most frequent crime victims were unsuspecting tourists with their fashions from other places, like wearing a tag on their foreheads that said, "I'm not from here." Their carelessness cost them their wallets and sometimes their lives.

As he exited the elevator, he greeted the young morning shift receptionist, who, besides smiling, looked him up and down. "That's how Uruguayan women look at a man when they are interested," Adrián thought." Without pretense or protocol. Directly in the eyes and then the rest of the body." Unlike in the United States, where staring at a stranger for more than a second in the subway or restaurant goes against social conventions. This stark contrast made the detective smile. He headed towards the corner of Avenida Brasil and Benito Blanco Street and sat in the same bar from his last visit, El Yoruga. He chose a table by the window and ordered his favorite breakfast, a long cappuccino, and a hot ham and cheese croissant. While waiting, he took his cell phone from his pocket and called Néstor Alonso, the doorman of the building where Sofía's sister lived. They agreed to meet in fifteen minutes as he was only three blocks away. He left the payment and tip on the table and walked down Gomensoro Square to the boardwalk. The sea was as smooth as a plate, and seagulls were chirping, gathered on the shore. The air smelled as if someone had been scaling fish on the rocks. A cargo ship approaching the port interrupted the horizon line. Adrián arrived at his destination fifteen minutes later. The Cabelas building, a sumptuous modern architectural structure, stood imposingly, surrounded by chalets with half-round tile roofs, dinosaurs from other times that the upper class had used as summer homes and still survived, stubborn, among the skyscrapers gradually conquering the traditional Riviera of Punta Carretas. The doorman was waiting for him at the door. Adrián wondered if, despite his precautions, he also had a sign on his forehead announcing he came from foreign lands because upon seeing him, the doorman extended his pale, bony hand before he introduced himself.

Néstor Alonso was a gray-looking man, with a head shaped like an egg, a few strands still fighting total baldness. Tiny eyes sunk beneath a short forehead where eyebrows were almost indistinguishable. An aquiline nose, flattened lips against the frame of a narrow mouth, and a prominent jaw gave this unattractive individual an almost medieval appearance. He must have been around sixty years old. He smelled of black coffee and onions from the sweat accumulated in his armpits. He wore a short-sleeved shirt from which hung hairy and muscular limbs, discordant with his scrawny torso. He had a black rose tattooed on his left forearm. His pale, saddened complexion reflected a fragility that contrasted with the firm grip with which he shook the detective's hand. On top of everything, he was hunchbacked. He walked ahead of Adrián towards the elevators with his right shoulder more inclined than the left, reinforcing his sickly appearance. The Penthouse was on the 32nd floor. A week had passed since the macabre discovery, and the police had already released the crime scene to the victim's immediate family, which consisted of only two people: her twenty-one-year-old son Javier and her sister Sofía. Upon entering, the yellow tapes placed by the experts were still visible, marking areas of possible evidence or fingerprints of the killer, as well as white chalk outlines on the parquet floor of the living room to delineate the position where the corpse had been found.

"That's where I found her. Poor Mrs. Carlota, mercilessly strangled by a monstrous man!"

"How do you know it was a man?"

"I suppose so, Mr. Fontana," the doorman reacted, quickly turning his pupils towards the detective. "The lady knew how to defend herself very well, and if it had been a woman, I don't think she would have succeeded."

Adrián knew more than one woman with enough strength to strangle another or even Alonso himself, but he said nothing.

"And why did you discover her?"

"The neighbor from the opposite Penthouse alerted me to a nauseating smell seeping under the door. Mrs. Carlota had left me an extra key to let in maintenance services when she was not home. I entered and there she lay, with her body twisted and swollen eyes staring at the ceiling, with a broken arm under her back."

"And how did you know it was broken if it was under the body, Alonso?"

The little man blinked twice and raised his eyes to Adrián, who was looking at him over his shoulder. He slightly raised his palm and said, "According to the police, the killer acted with such bloody violence that he broke her arm before strangling her." He raised his eyebrows in a mourning posture and with languid, lost eyes added, "Poor unfortunate, she was so beautiful!"

Adrián didn't need Alonso to describe Carlota's physical beauty. He had known her very well during the first six months he worked at one of her father's factories and later when he dated Sofía.

"Is the apartment still as you found it?"

"Of course, Mr. Fontana, I didn't touch anything, and no one else has entered since the police released the crime scene to the family. I don't know if the experts took anything for laboratory analysis, but from what I see, everything is in its usual place. Yesterday, Mrs. Carlota's son called me and said he would come by today or tomorrow to check that nothing of value was taken, especially the paintings, which, according to him, are worth a fortune."

Adrián continued touring the Penthouse while Alonso followed closely. In the bedroom, the bed was impeccably made. On the kitchen table were two empty whiskey bottles, which did not surprise him. He knew Carlota was an alcoholic; she had been since her first divorce at the age of twenty, and despite her parents' efforts, who had interned her in the most prestigious private clinics in the capital, her addiction had only known intervals but always resurrected like the Phoenix. He returned to the living room and scanned the walls adorned with oils by national painting masters. There were also some foreign ones. Adrián had always been interested in the visual arts, which did not quite rhyme with the rest of his apparent insensitivity. All were hung in perfect symmetry, maximizing the space. Given their substantial value, he thought perhaps robbery was not the motive for the crime. He especially remembered the oil painting of the white wolf, which Donato Ferraro proudly displayed like a hunting trophy in his Carrasco mansion. The white wolf drinking at the edge of a stream under the full moon in a European forest. It had impressed him since the first time he saw it displayed in Donato Ferraro's billiard room. It had been painted in the nineteenth century by a Polish artist, and the old man had acquired it at an auction in Hamburg during one of his trips to the old world. In the upper right corner, a small piece of paint had chipped off, showing some cracks near the full moon, but according to experts, it was easily restorable, and as it was, it was appraised years later at eighty thousand dollars. Don Ferraro had paid twenty thousand, which for him was a bargain in his glory days. Adrián knew Carlota had always coveted that painting, and he was surprised not to see it on the Penthouse walls. He was aware that the deceased had appropriated all the family's art heritage after the old man died.

"What happened to the white wolf painting?" he asked casually, studying Alonso's body language.

"White wolf painting?" said the doorman, scratching his neck. "I don't pay much attention to those things, Mr. Fontana. I'm an ignorant man; art is not my thing," replied the hunchback. He paused briefly and massaged his chin. Then he added, "Oh, wait . . . now that you mention it . . . I think there was a painting of a wolf on that wall. Was it a large painting, wasn't it? Like twice the size of that one?" he asked, pointing to a Torres García.

"Yes, much larger."

"Look at that . . . I have a vague memory of something like that . . . ; Do you think the killer took it?"

"I have no idea, Alonso, but I'm glad I refreshed your memory."

The doorman shrugged and drew a silly smile without acknowledging the sarcasm.

"How interesting, Mr. Fontana, that might be a good lead for Commissioner Bermúdez!"

"Do you know who visited Mrs. Carlota, Alonso?"

"Not many people came, at least as far as I know. Sometimes her son and lately a woman missing her right arm visited her. Mrs. Carlota called her Lucrecia. She had a Spanish accent and wasn't very friendly. She spoke to Mrs. Carlota with an air of superiority."

"Anyone else?"

"The truth is, I don't know for sure. A lot of people pass through this hall, and not everyone says where they are going."

"Well, that's all for now. Thank you for showing me the apartment. If you remember anything else, please call me."

He extended his hand and again felt the firm grip of the doorman, who accompanied the greeting with a brief smile without parting his lips.

As he stepped onto the street, Adrián lit a cigarette and walked slowly along the boardwalk towards Buceo's little port. He took a deep breath of the salt air carried by the coastal breeze, still fresh from the sun. It was 10:15 in the morning. As the cigarette continued to shrink between his lips, he thought about Sofía again. Why had she chosen him to investigate her sister's death? This time, the answer came clear as crystal. She was a practical and intelligent woman. She knew he knew the family history in detail, which gave him an advantage over any other investigator. "It's a calculated decision," he told himself. "There is no sentimental motivation in the offer, in case you get any illusions, Fontana."

# V

DONATO FERRARO HAD BUILT a food industry empire with headquarters in Montevideo and branches throughout the rest of the country. At fifteen, he left high school and began delivering fresh and canned groceries by bicycle in the city of Rocha. Ten years later, his trucks were already distributing merchandise throughout rural Uruguay, and he was on his way to becoming the most powerful wholesaler outside the capital. He covered almost all food and beverage categories commonly seen on grocery store shelves. He then bought a bankrupt canned goods factory and a sausage manufacturing plant in the city of Canelones that had succumbed to union strikes. He was not intimidated by leftists; he knew how to deal with them. Back then, any businessman who crossed his giant path and had previously fallen into disgrace, perished crushed. He was married to Renata Fonseca, a girl from his neighborhood, the daughter of a modest carpenter, who lived in the train station district. Sofía always recounted how her mother told her about the beginning of their courtship. Donato was playing a pickup soccer game with his neighborhood friends on the street. The young Renata approached the group on the sidewalk, heading to the butcher shop. As she passed by the boys, the compliments rained down. Some were artistically creative, but others spouted vulgarities about the girl's curves. They forgot about the rag ball and surrounded her, whispering obscenities in her ear. Donato intervened between the girl and the boldest of the group.

"That's enough, Garufa. Leave her alone!" he said. Nothing more was needed. The group studied the determined look of the railway worker's son, who already had his fists ready, and that was enough for them. They knew it wasn't a good idea to provoke the burly boy.

"Allow me to accompany you, miss. This way, you can avoid any problems with these fools on your way back," he suggested to the girl, taking off his cap in accordance with the custom of the time of not addressing each other informally at the first meeting. She smiled. The rest happened effortlessly. "Love at first sight," as Renata Fonseca would tell her daughter. Six months later, they got married, and in 1950, when Donato outgrew the city of Rocha, they moved to Montevideo with Carlota, who had just turned one. It was then that the carpenter's daughter decided to stop being simply Renata when she visited the capital's banks, dressed in the luxuries of the time, to request a loan for the company.

"Tell the manager that I am Doña Renata Fonseca de Ferraro and that he should hurry. I'm not used to waiting! Banks and low-interest financing are plentiful nowadays," she said, raising her chin.

Adrián knew all these stories from Sofía. He delighted in his girlfriend's impressions of her mother when they dined years later in their Turner Street apartment on the hill of Church Hill in Richmond, Virginia.

In 1980, when he still didn't know Sofía, by a capricious coincidence of fate, Adrián started working at a cardboard box factory. Renato Ferraro had bought it to package some of the products he distributed. By then, his firm had been established for over thirty years and covered not only the entire national territory but also exported to southern Brazil, Argentina, and Chile. The man from Rocha continued moving at lightning speed. Adrián worked as an operator of Olivetti computers, those enormous plastic dinosaurs, pioneers of business computing. He and Tomás, his coworker, were isolated from the rest of the staff in air-conditioned glass cages, wearing their impeccable white gowns as required by the corporate dress code of the time for the computing department employees. Their colleagues called them "the cyber doctors." The machines had transparent cassettes the size of a book, with magnetic tapes that snaked inside, recording all the data memory required for accounting, invoicing, stock control, or whatever was needed. The old bookkeepers were starting to look at them with suspicion. They could smell unemployment in the air. Where ten were needed before, now two sufficed. One morning, Adrián was changing one of the cassettes when he saw Carlota for the first time through the glass cubicle.

"Who's that?" he asked.

"Carlota Ferraro, the boss's eldest daughter," Tomás replied cautiously, covering his words with his hand.

"She's got a good figure."

"Yes, she's hot, but it's better to lose her than win her. She's as bad as a rabid dog! I've seen her humiliate and break the strongest spirits here in the office. Some have come out of her office crying."

She walked through the aisles formed by the desks lined up like a general inspecting her troops. She had slim but firm and well-shaped legs. She walked with an elastic and relaxed step. Her backside drew a slight, not excessive curve, in harmony with the other curve that stood in the opposite direction, the one marked by her breasts. She had red hair, neither very long nor very short, discreetly scattered freckles around her straight nose, a firm and haughty gaze, and a barely fleshy mouth that she pressed in a gesture at odds with a smile. She walked with the grace of elegant high-society women, but there was no sign of feminine tenderness in her Napoleonic stride. After surveying all those unfortunate people, with their heads bowed, anchored to their desks, she headed toward the stairs leading to the second floor where the boardroom was located.

"Nice, Cleopatra's parade, but she's not my type, man," Adrián commented indifferently as he resumed typing on the Olivetti. He had survived six months and was the first to be surprised. In those days, he didn't last long in any job due to his volatile temperament. In the neighborhood, they called him "tin kettle" because he heated up quickly. Except for attractive and uncomplicated women, he was an oddball who didn't get along with anyone. Not the bosses, not the sycophants. Not the fascists or communists, not the old resentful people or the overly optimistic ones. The only exception was his mother, whom he saw as a saint dedicated to him and others, always finding the good side of things. He hated the office routine but was determined to endure it for six more months until he saved enough to travel to the United States. He had wanted to study criminology since he was a child, and the fantasy still lingered.

# VI

Forty-eight hours had passed since Adrián's arrival in Montevideo. It was nine in the morning, and he was sitting in El Yoruga waiting for breakfast, which was much tastier than what the hotel offered. He was at the table by the window, a spot always available at that hour of the day. He entertained himself by watching people pass by while awaiting the arrival of "Rabbit" Vergara, his friend from preparatory school. There was plenty to see. An old man being dragged by a great Dane, panting as he chased the canine horse, making it impossible to tell who was walking whom. A domestic worker in an apron, cap, and humble clothes that didn't match the neighborhood swept the sidewalk across the street, and a bit further back, a chubby lady made a face of disgust with her painted lips as she looked at her shoe smeared with dog poop, the kind that abounds on the sidewalks of Pocitos. Adrián's eyes were fixed on the curves of a stunning brunette passing by the window when he felt a pat on the back. He turned around, and there was "Rabbit" Vergara, who had snuck in to surprise him with his usual smile, generous teeth brushing his lower lip.

"How are you, brother, so many years! How long has it been since we last saw each other, Adrián?"

"Only two, you fool, since my mother died," said the detective, hugging him tightly.

Rubén Vergara, alias Rabbit, was the son of the late Commissioner José Vergara, a legend in the fight against capital crime, who had been politically respected by fascists, communists, and anarchists in the seventies before the coup d'état. He was a tough cop but didn't have a twisted soul. His son had turned out a bit softer but more cunning and ingenious than his father in maintaining all the Commissioner's contacts. After his progenitor's death, he moved around the Montevideo scene, inside and outside the Central Intelligence unit of the police headquarters as if he were the commissioner. Astute in bribes, which were an institution throughout the republic, he knew how to reward favors with voluminous crates of imported whiskey, luxuries afforded by his generous salary as an accountant at the State Insurance Bank. Rabbit Vergara was six-foot-three. He had extremely long legs relative to his torso and a bit of a big butt, which added to his peculiar appearance. His physique wasn't athletic but not too overweight except for his hips where fat accumulated. This sometimes caused his shirt to come untucked, and Rabbit, who was extremely vain, would hurriedly tuck it back in.

A staunch bachelor but never short of female company. His exuberant and boisterous personality made many women feel attracted to the big guy with a goofy look and found it fascinating to go out with him. They knew fun and night partying were guaranteed. He had a husky voice and spoke excessively loudly, but he didn't seem to notice unless someone pointed it out. A small gap between his front teeth caused words to come out with a whistling lisp that didn't harmonize with his imposing figure.

"Thanks for coming, Vergara. Sorry I didn't bring a carrot to sharpen those front incisors."

"Go to hell, asshole!" said the booming voice, with the "s" in "asshole" sounding like a "z."

"Asshole isn't spelled with a 'z,' you moron," said the detective. He enjoyed teasing him. Their conversations had always been like this, and they both endured the jokes.

"Since school, with the same joke, change the repertoire!" said Rabbit, rolling his eyes.

"Don't get mad, Rabbit. You know deep down I care about you. Anyway, spill it . . . What do you know about Commissioner Bermúdez?"

"Bermúdez is a chicken cop who swims with the current and knows how to cozy up to the warmest sun, but he's not a dangerous guy," said Rabbit, raising his hand. When the waiter approached, he ordered a Coke with ice and a dulce de leche pastry.

"But . . . Do you think he's seriously investigating the crime?"

"He'll investigate as long as it doesn't implicate any of his buddies."

"Like whom? Come on, spill it, don't keep me in suspense."

"Adrián, did you know your ex-sister-in-law was involved with Cheeks Stern, who, on top of that, is

Bermúdez's daughter's godfather? Your ex-sister-in-law didn't mess around. Do you know who Cheeks is?"

"Stop calling her my sister-in-law, idiot, I never married her sister."

"Yeah, but you were close. What happened? You never told me."

"Don't bust my balls, Rabbit. I don't talk about my stuff. Come on, continue! And lower your voice, people can hear us from a block away," said Adrián, putting a finger to his lips.

"Okay, fine 'Tin kettle,' don't blow a gasket," said Rabbit, laughing, raising his arms, "It was just friendly curiosity."

"Come on, Rabbit, stick to the main topic, or there'll be no carrot."

"Do you know or not who 'Cheeks' Stern is?" insisted Rabbit, now lowering his tone, leaning across the table, and widening his eyes.

"Of course I know, you fourth-rate idiot! The son of 'The Beard' Stern. Do I look like I was born yesterday? They're more famous than Al Capone and were already famous when I left thirteen years ago."

"Dale."

"Dale what? What's this 'dale' I've been hearing since I got off the plane?"

"It's the latest fad imported from Argentina, 'Tin Kettle,' don't get worked up," said Rabbit after another loud, husky laugh that turned more than one head. "The Porteños always come up with some new saying, and we love to copy them. It's like the 'OK' from the Americans or the 'vale' from the Spaniards. Get it? I finish a sentence, and you say, 'dale,' meaning OK. If I invite you for a whiskey, you answer 'dale.' The kids started it, and now everyone uses it, got it?" said the big guy, biting his tongue with a mocking gesture.

"Dale, you idiot! Continue."

"Dale! Well, if you know Cheeks, you'll know you must be careful because that fat guy is bad and will have you taken out without blinking," warned Rabbit while turning around to look at a girl's butt as she headed for the exit.

The waiter brought their order. Adrián poured three packets of sugar into his cappuccino and stirred it slowly not to break the foam. Rabbit Vergara bit one end of the pastry, and the dulce de leche overflowed onto his lip. He wiped his mouth with his finger and licked it.

"Tell me . . . what happened to Yamandú Bonilla?" continued Adrián. "Is he still on active duty? When I came with Sofía to Don Ferraro's funeral in 1990, Carlota had the lieutenant colonel standing to her right like a guard dog, baring his teeth."

"Damn! Your sister-in-law was quite something, I didn't know she was also involved with Bonilla!"

"Call her my sister-in-law again, and I'll take your teeth back to Richmond as a souvenir. Come on, what do you know about Bonilla?"

"That he's like a rabid dog, cornered by the press and the courts. They're closing in on him with accusations of torture from the dictatorship era. There's a historical revisionism, and many retired military officers are starting to be prosecuted. Look, Adrián, if your sister . . . I mean, Carlota, hehe," he paused, "was involved first with Bonilla and then with Cheeks Stern, she was playing with fire, and I can only help you up to a point. You know the Sterns were friends of my old man, and Cheeks sometimes invites me to his barbecues. I don't want trouble with him."

"Don't worry, Vergara, I'm not going to ruin your party. What you've told me for now is enough. Go on, you're going to be late for work, and they'll scold you."

"I don't have a set time, I come and go as I please," he replied, self-sufficiently. "Oh, I almost forgot, Adrián, I have a place on Sierra Street, near the Retirement fund building. If you get lucky with any girl, let me know, and I'll give you the key, okay?"

"Okay, King of the Night! Thanks for the offer. And what do you do there, masturbate? Because with that face, who's going to pay attention to you," the detective commented, showing he was holding back laughter.

"You got it right. The King of the Night! Well, I'm off," said Rabbit, wiping his mouth with the napkin, "but you know, take it easy. I don't want trouble with the big shots, okay?"

"Yeah, okay, okay!"

"Okay!" taunted the lanky guy as he left, making silly movements with his body.

# VII

LORENZO "THE BEAR" STERN was a Jewish mobster, the patriarch of the newspaper and magazine vendors' union, and the carnival's troupes. He was also one of the leading figures in national horse racing. He raised several famous racehorses that shone at the Maroñas racetrack and international events. Those who admired him called him "the caudillo of the newsboys." He had eliminated the competition with an iron fist and at gunpoint. There wasn't a kiosk in downtown Montevideo or the most remote suburb that didn't pay the stipulated monthly fee in exchange for the supposed protection against crime offered by his henchmen. Those who paid kept their kiosks. Those who rebelled ended up floating in the black waters of the Miguelete stream or with their faces disfigured by the union's thugs.

Adrián had met old Stern once when his father took him to one of the men-only fishing clubs nestled among the rocks of Ramírez beach. There, feasts and drunken parties were organized, bankrolled by the caudillo. Amid the merriment of glasses and laughter, through the haze of smoke created by the smokers, the Jew appeared with his son, nicknamed Cheeks, who at that time would have been about twenty-two years old. Everyone fell silent. The sycophants tripped over themselves to offer him a chair. A mangy cat approached Cheeks and began to rub against his pants. It let out a shrill meow when Cheeks kicked it away. Everyone laughed out of obligation except Adrián, who approached angrily and delivered a vigorous kick to his shins. The hefty son of the caudillo winced and frowned.

"Who is this little shit, and where did he come from?" he reacted, brandishing his right fist. Adrián, who didn't even reach his waist, began throwing punches at him.

No one laughed, except old Stern, who broke the ice with a hearty laugh. Seeing his father's reaction,

Cheeks relaxed. He extended his arm and placed his large hand on the child's forehead, who continued throwing punches in the air without being able to advance towards the tower that stopped him. The old patriarch lit a cigar, approached Adrián, patted his head, and commented to the bricklayer, "Nice boy. He looks like a little fighting cock!" Then he disappeared with his son among the crowd of sycophants that followed them like lapdogs.

"Who is that man?" Adrián asked, still red with anger in his face.

"That is Lorenzo 'The Bear' Stern, a man very beloved by all the newsboys," said the bricklayer. The child waited for a reprimand for his audacity, but his father added nothing. Deep down, he was proud of the little one.

Adrián never saw old Stern again. However, as a teenager, he often saw the successor to the throne, Alberto "Cheeks" Stern, surrounded by women in Montevideo's nightclubs or leading his Carnival troupe La Nueva Milonga, parading down 18 de Julio Avenue. He was nicknamed Cheeks because, as a child, he had fleshy, exuberant, and glossy red chubby cheeks, physical traits he still maintained in adulthood. "Cheeks"

Stern, who like his father was an obese giant of enormous stature, had inherited his father's domain after the latter collapsed from a heart attack in the stands of the Maroñas racetrack, screaming like a madman for the victory of Sol de Noche. He didn't have his father's charismatic virtues. However, he surpassed him in violence and sadism. The newsboys rumored that at the age of 16, old Stern had sent him to New York to disappear for a while until things calmed down. The young gangster had castrated a mulatto who bled to death for stealing his girlfriend. This local mafia gem had been in bed with Carlota Ferraro, and despite the cautious advice of "Rabbit" Vergara, Adrián intended to find out if Carlota's strangled neck had succumbed under Cheeks's claws or one of his thugs. It wouldn't have surprised him, given the nature of the crime, but before investigating Stern's escapades, he had another visit to make that Thursday afternoon.

# VIII

THE DETECTIVE HAD TWO visits on his agenda: Javier, the victim's son, and Lucrecia Contreras, the art dealer Alonso had mentioned. He decided to start with the latter, perhaps because of his inclination toward the arts or because the insolent, spoiled brat of barely twenty years of age easily got on his nerves ever since he was a child. He had called "Rabbit" Vergara to find Lucrecia Contreras' address. A one-armed art dealer was not the most common sight in the Montevideo market. His friend didn't find it difficult to get him the information. The gallery was located near Plaza Independencia. He walked down the narrow side-walks of Bartolomé Mitre, the cobblestone street that descended from Artigas' plaza towards the port's waterfront.

The gallery was housed in a building with a colonial facade, featuring a double carved pine door and wrought iron balconies adorned with ferns and geraniums. The door was wide open, giving way to a frosted glass inner door that chimed as he entered the gallery. It was a rectangular and elongated space, not very well-lit except for the spotlights on the ceiling aimed at the oil paintings hanging on both sides of the central aisle. At the back, what seemed to be two clients were animatedly conversing with a woman in her fifties, wrapped in a thick green corduroy blazer, with the right sleeve hanging flat and lifeless like a scarf by her side.

While waiting, he walked along the walls where the works of the greatest national painters were displayed: Figari's blacks, Blanes Viale's purple landscapes, Lussich's gauchos, and Torres García's sad and almost monochromatic geometries. He was intently studying the thick brushstrokes of a Blanes Viale oil painting when he heard the hoarse voice of the woman in her fifties bidding farewell to the couple. She accompanied them to the door and then turned her knife-like eyes towards the detective.

"Nice to meet you, Mr. Fontana. Congratulations! A guy coming from the land of the blondes in the north, with a wallet full of greens, and looking with an expert eye. That Blanes Viale is striking, isn't it?"

Adrián smiled and shook her already extended left hand. The woman studied him with her opaque black pupils. Her hair was ash-colored, almost shaved, with a barely suggested fringe on her forehead. Her nose was slightly hooked like that of a gypsy. Her thin-lipped mouth formed a twisted, disdainful smirk when she spoke. Her body language did not match her physical disability as she stood before the detective as if he were her chauffeur.

"The truth is, I first wanted to see your face, but if we are going to talk about Carlota, let me close the shop and invite you for a drink in my apartment, where we can talk more quietly. It's close by, two blocks away, in the Palacio Salvo. Does that sound good to you?"

"Yes, okay. Whatever you prefer, Miss Contreras."

"Just call me Lucrecia; I'm not as respectable as I look," she replied, letting out a raspy laugh that evidenced many hours of alcohol and partying.

To him, she didn't seem respectable, but since he couldn't confess that, he simply said: "Okay, Lucrecia."

The Palacio Salvo had been one of the tallest towers in South America at the time of its inauguration in 1928, with an eclectic Art Deco style that combined Renaissance references with Gothic reminiscences and some neoclassical touches. The basement garage had once housed a theater where personalities like Jorge Negrete and Josephine Baker had performed. It was approximately 100 meters high with 29 floors of grand proportions. To its left was the Government House, in the center the colossal statue of Artigas, farther back the Solís Theater, and to the right the luxurious Victoria Plaza Hotel, a haven for artists and heads of state visiting the city.

Lucrecia Contreras lived on the 17th floor. Upon entering, she unbuttoned her blazer, tilted her left shoulder, slightly contorted her body, and with a quick, precise movement pulled the bottom edge with her only arm, deftly freeing herself from the coat as if by routine. Her semi-circular apartment offered a privileged 180-degree view, covering the center of the old city, the port with its enormous container plaza, cargo ships, and luxury cruise ships. In the distance, across the vast bay, the white spot of the Montevideo Hill fortress could be seen, which supposedly gave the city its name. "Monte vi Eu," legend says a Portuguese sailor exclaimed during the exploration of the Río de la Plata by the old-world empires. Following the four balconies arranged in a semicircle, with threatening gargoyles perched on their edges, one could see the Palermo promenade and then the curve where Punta Carretas began.

The detective praised the prodigious view of the city and then the magnificent watercolor by Esteban Garino hanging in the spacious living room. All the furniture exuded classic museum decor, except for the smell of marijuana that the incense sticks lit by the homeowner couldn't quite overcome. Beside the armchair, there was a monumental, black-mouthed stove. Inside, a thick iron wood burner stood on four legs resembling lion's claws.

Adrián leaned back against the balcony facing the port, with a glass of Johnny Walker Black Label in his left hand and a Nevada cigarette in his right, his preferred brand when traveling to Uruguay. Standing in the doorway, the Spaniard smoked a Marlboro clamped at the side of her mouth, alternating it with a generous glass of vodka placed on a folding table next to the window. She placed the cigarette in the ashtray, grabbed the glass, drank halfway, then put it back on the table, and returned to the cigarette.

"This thing of doing everything with the left hand, it's shit, man!"

"How did you lose the other one?"

"That was when I still believed in love, handsome. Twenty years ago, I was deeply involved with a Greek woman who one day left looking for younger flesh, and I decided to throw myself under a train," she said, twisting her lips. "You know I'm a dyke. I could tell from your face when you shook my hand at the gallery."

Adrián smiled and replied, raising his eyebrows: "You can tell these things, Lucrecia; besides, I have a trained eye from the profession."

The one-armed woman laughed, stubbed out the cigarette, and downed the other half of the glass. "Want another Scotch, handsome?"

"Well, if you insist."

"Do you stick with Johnny, or should I pour you a Chivas?"

"I'd rather stick with Johnny Black. We've been friends for years, and I don't want to betray him."

"That's the spirit, I see you're not a racist," she reacted with another fierce, raspier laugh than before.

She headed to the crystal bar where she had a collection of alcohol for all tastes: Johnny Walker red, black, and blue, Don Cuervo Tequila, Belvedere Vodka, Four Roses Bourbon, and all kinds of international spirits. She generously filled the glasses and continued with the story.

"I miscalculated, and the damn train hit me on the side. It only ripped off my arm. Life didn't matter a damn, so I decided to become a war correspondent for El País, in Madrid. I made some money interviewing every bastard breathing in the Middle East, the Balkans, or anywhere else where humanity was tearing itself apart. One day, I got tired of dodging death and came to taste pussy in the Río de la Plata basin. Let's not waste time on niceties, handsome, hahaha."

"No drama, Lucrecia, to call a spade a spade. How did the hunt go in the southern seas?"

"Great, man! Montevideo is rich in women willing to come out of the closet, though you men are completely unaware. This city is a goldmine where creoles play both sides: with their husbands and me abound."

"That's great, Lucrecia! This is all very educational and enriching. You have the same adventurous spirit as the ancient conquerors of the Spanish Empire and have come to establish the Lesbian Viceroyalty of the Río de la Plata. How did you end up as an art dealer?"

"That's another story. I'm not going to tell you about my whole life in just one damn night, you bastard," she laughed as she returned to the bar to refill her glass. Then she said: "So, according to you, Carlota's sister hired you to investigate the crime."

"That's right. How did you meet Carlota?"

"It was at the gallery. I sold one of her paintings. The poor woman was desperate for cash when her company collapsed."

"The painting of the white wolf?"

They stared at each other in a duel of eyes where the first to blink would lose.

"Very well, Mr. Detective, I see you're well informed about the deceased's artistic heritage, but I'm sorry to disappoint you, handsome. No, it wasn't the white wolf. I always wanted to buy that one, but she refused. One day, during one of my visits to the penthouse, I didn't see it hanging, and I got furious with her. She told me she had sold it without consulting me, but I never bought that story."

"Why not?"

"This market is small, and everything is known. Such a sale would eventually come to light. I would have found out. I thought she might have it hidden or stored elsewhere for some reason."

"And did you visit her only for art-related reasons or also for other reasons?"

The one-armed woman laughed again and replied: "I wanted to take her to bed more than once, but Carlota was very insecure, full of prejudices and complexes, too cowardly to experiment. I suppose you don't have that problem, handsome. So many years in Gringoland must have opened your mind, I hope . . ." she laughed again.

"Did you ever find out who bought the wolf painting?"

"She never wanted to tell me, the bitch; shall I pour you another Johnny?"

"Sure."

She returned with the refilled glass. Adrián remained leaning against the balcony. As she handed him the glass, the one-armed woman stumbled and ended up pressed against the detective's body. For a split second, Adrián's first thought was that the vodka was taking effect, and she had lost her balance. This thought clarified immediately when he felt her knee rubbing his groin.

"Oops! I miscalculated again," she said with glossy eyes, her alcoholic breath close to him. "As I told you, I'm kind of clumsy and uncoordinated when it comes to measuring distances."

No more was needed. Adrián was a good connoisseur of erotic advances. He reacted with a smug smile while instinctively pulling his face back a few centimeters. Now that Lucrecia no longer had the glass in her hand, she used it to replace her knee, grabbing firmly the contents behind his fly.

"Hey, hey! You're moving too fast, my friend," said Adrián, raising his arm.

She insisted on advancing, seeing the look of hesitation reflected in the detective's furrowed brow, which was now starting to form an ironic smile. She reinforced the attack by winking and raising her eyebrows twice without pause, inviting him.

"I can still do wonders. With my mouth and one hand, it's enough," said the art dealer, swiftly sliding the tip of her tongue over her upper lip.

Adrián was aware she was a pervert, but still, the proposition caught him off guard. He arched his eyebrows and squinted his eyes while asking: "But . . . wasn't it that you batted for the other team?"

"I already told you, I like to experiment, dumbass! Come on, take off your pants," she almost begged now like a pampered cat. "I want to suck your cock before I go pass out drunk. Lesbian by vocation, but I also do other gigs, baby."

"Here we call them 'tortilleras.'"

"Tortilleras, 'bolleras,' or 'dikes' in English, I don't give a damn about synonyms. Stop stalling and take off your pants, bastard!" she exploded, now enraged.

"Calm down, Marchand . . . don't let the Belvedere vodka awaken your aggressiveness. Slow down, my friend. Let's keep talking about Carlota. What else do you know about her?"

"Are you one of those queers who haven't come out of the closet yet?"

"Exactly! You discovered my secret, darling. Let's continue with Carlota, and then we'll see if I make an effort and overcome my homosexuality to accept your generous offer."

"'After we'll see,' my ass! Get out, I'm sick of you, pig! I'm going to bed. Close the door when you leave," she snapped, slurring her words soaked in Smirnoff.

She turned around and left, performing dance pirouettes, moving with her arm raised and waving the drug-filled glass. The right sleeve fluttered like a curtain in the wind with her dance steps.

Adrián downed the Johnny Walker in one gulp, opened the door, and left the Medusa's lair. He regretted not being Perseus and taking the monster's head in his hand.

# IX

THERE WERE FOUR PEOPLE listening to the pastor's words, arranged in a semicircle around the Ferraro family mausoleum in the Central Cemetery. To Adrián's left was Consuelo, the housemaid who had served three generations of the Ferraro family. She sobbed as if her body were a huge reservoir of tears with a leak in her eyes. On his right, standing like a stone statue, was Javier Ferraro, Carlota's natural son, and then Sofía at the end of the line.

Adrián felt the pastor's speech as distant. His senses were focused solely on Sofía. Why the hell couldn't she at least be there, holding his hand? He cursed fate and Javier's body that separated him from her, but he knew the answer. He had been an idiot, and sometimes there are no second chances.

His ex-girlfriend stood on the grass with dignified, sad beauty. He assumed her wet eyes were contemplating Carlota's final destination, comparing the past and present of the Ferraro family. Perhaps she remembered when she was five years old and saw her father running out in his underwear late at night, chasing promiscuous Carlota, who had just turned thirteen, sneaking out of the Carrasco mansion to meet her latest boyfriend, or who knows which of the many other stories Sofía had told him were now running through her head as it hung over the grave.

Contaminated also by memories of youth, he escaped to the cardboard factory, the first time he saw Sofía.

"Who's that cutie, Tomás?" He had asked his coworker.

"Sofía, the boss's youngest daughter. She doesn't look anything like her sister, neither physically nor mentally. Paradoxes of genetics. Both raised in the same house, the eldest a terrible bitch and the other, a saint. The employees adore her. Carlota and her mother say that if Sofía had her way, she would cover all her father's factories with carpeting so the workers could better endure standing on the conveyor belts. They call her 'Sofía, the lyrical.'

He listened intently to Tomás's story while his eyes traveled over the fresh, student-like figure approaching the Olivetti cage. She had an air of Maria Schneider, the protagonist of *Last Tango in Paris*. A mane of tousled curls, a softly rounded face where proportionate eyebrows rested, almond shaped honey-colored eyes, a cute nose that sometimes wrinkled in a mischievous hippie gesture, and a heart-shaped mouth painted blood red that matched her olive complexion. She wore a tight blue t-shirt that accentuated her well-proportioned breasts, with a large bright yellow sun with sequins on its rays that reflected light in all directions. A wide leather belt further reduced her narrow waist and highlighted her moderately curvy hips that she moved with unstudied grace.

Her jet-black skirt was a tube that clung to just past her knee, complemented by medium-heeled shoes of the same color.

"Hi, Tomás, I don't know your colleague. I'm Sofía Ferraro. Are you new to the company?" the young woman smiled, with her mouth and eyes.

"Nice to meet you. My name is Adrián Fontana," he responded, extending his hand. "I started six months ago. I haven't seen you before either. Are you new too?" he joked.

She laughed, acknowledging the humor and clarified: "Lately I haven't come to the factory much because of university exams.

"Oh, what are you studying?"

"Law. International Law," she answered enthusiastically.

"That's great, congratulations!"

"Well, welcome to the factory, Adrián. See you around. I'm going up. The big boss is waiting for me. Now that I'm on vacation, today I start working part-time as secretary for grumpy don Ferraro."

"Well, let's be clear, you're the one saying that as his daughter, not me who wants to keep my job here in the cage."

She laughed, turned around, and walked her firm and curvy buttocks bound by the tube skirt towards the stairs leading to the second floor. Before stepping on the first stair, she slightly turned her head to check her female intuition and found Adrián's eyes still on her. Her lips curled mischievously, and she began the ascent to her father's office.

In those days, Adrián Fontana was discreetly successful in his romantic escapades, but when he met Sofía, his script got complicated. Now, the girls flirting with him were neutralized by the image of Sofía that had anchored itself in his mind, both inside and outside the office, or lying down looking at his bedroom ceiling.

A month after their first meeting, Adrián invited her for coffee at La Pasiva, located in the romantic Plaza Matriz, under the pretext of helping him prepare for some English exams. He arrived late because the bus was delayed. Sofía was waiting for him, sitting with a lit cigarette. She blew long clouds into the air without inhaling the smoke, like young women who haven't been smoking for many years. Her hair was tied back tightly, parted in the middle, with a flamenco bun that highlighted the grace of her neck. Adding to the charm were gypsy earrings and perfectly blended purple shadows on her eyelids. Precisely lined on her lips shone a crimson red that left its mark on the filter of the menthol L&M.

"Sorry I'm late. The bus driver was like a tortoise!"

"It's okay, but don't make it a habit," she smiled.

Adrián stared at her, comparing her attire and hairstyle with the hippie girl look from their first meeting.

"Perfect, the transformation from Maria Schneider to Bizet's Carmen! I have the most beautiful gypsy in all of Andalusia in front of me!"

"Andalusian, only on my mother's side," she clarified, raising her index finger with a spontaneous girlish laugh. "Italian by my father's genes."

"Well then, Gina Lollobrigida or Claudia Cardinale."

"What an exaggeration! The pretty one in my family has always been Carlota."

Adrián explored the watercolor-like amber of the young woman's iris. She responded in kind with her eyes, and they stayed that way, their retinas mesmerized until the waiter came to take their order. They spent the last lights of the afternoon with English books and notebooks spread out on the table. She focused on Anglo-Saxon grammar, and he on the movement and shape of her mouth. When the sun set, they finished the lesson. She wanted to pay the bill, but Adrián didn't let her. Then he walked her to her car.

"Come on, get in. I'll treat you to an ice cream at Conaprole in Pocitos, okay? Then I'll drive you home."

Adrián didn't resist. As they walked along the waterfront, savoring the last pieces of ice cream cone, a storm of wind and torrential rain broke out as if the world were ending. Adrián took her hand to cross the dimly lit boulevard. The downpour slashed through the fleeting and blurry headlights of the cars, revealing the density of the rain. They took refuge in a gazebo next to the stairs of Plaza Gomensoro. Soaked, he lowered her hood and cupped her face with unknown tenderness. She impulsively stretched up to his six feet and kissed him lightly, almost timidly. They looked at each other transparently for a few seconds. Then, they melted into a prolonged kiss while the atomized water cooled their flushed cheeks.

After attending her sister's wake, Sofía stayed in Montevideo for twenty-four hours. Adrián took her to the airport and gave her a summary of what he knew so far while they had breakfast in the café. When the plane took off, the detective watched the Boeing 747 grow smaller in the sky until it disappeared among the clouds. He remained staring at the sky until the loudspeaker announcement of the next departure brought him back to the terminal. He lit a cigarette and headed to the parking lot. At eleven, he had an appointment with a woman who knew many secrets of the Ferraro family.

# X

"How are you, Mr. Adrián? What a joy to see you!" exclaimed Consuelo Flores, who had been waiting for the detective while seated in a discreet corner of El Yoruga bar.

She bore the simple, servile expression common to many women in her profession. She was gaunt, with such fine skin that her veins stood out swollen like behind a veil, on a face that suggested misfortune or frustration. A life of trampled dreams. Her cheek-bones inflated the discreet oval of her face. She had mouse-like eyes, timid but sharp. She always kept her neck retracted between her shoulders, with her head slightly inclined forward, a posture possibly acquired from occupational hazard. She had faithfully served and endured the Ferraro family for three generations. She had lived in Montevideo since she was fifteen, after having worked in one of the distribution branches that Donato Ferraro owned in the town of Aguas Quietas, in the Rio Negro department. The magnate had brought her to Montevideo to bolster the team of servants at his residence in Carrasco. Renata Fonseca Ferraro's nouveau riche whims increased daily, now requiring at least two maids and a cook. One for the heavy cleaning, another for laundry, ironing, and caring for her daughters, and the cook to prepare a varied menu to satisfy her husband's insatiable appetite when he came back from the factory.

The slender girl began her early military training under Renata's yoke. Over time, she witnessed all the storms and passions that brewed in the Carrasco mansion. Donato's marital infidelities. Renata's jealous scenes over her husband's excessive attention and weakness for their eldest daughter. Mother and daughter competed furiously for the patriarch's attention and love, sometimes venting their anger and frustrations on Consuelo or the other domestic staff. The servants whispered during siesta time, in the kitchen, that Donato perversely played with both, twisting his maneuvers and affections as it suited his interests. Consuelo's only oxygen was when she was alone with Sofía and could smile at her fresh teenage antics. Then it was her turn to play mother to Javier, Carlota's son, when she got pregnant after a brief affair with a former Green Beret turned mercenary who was passing through Montevideo. According to the version Carlota later confided to her friends, which spread like wildfire among Montevideo's elites and the servants' secret gatherings, Bobby, "just Bobby," had been the only true love of her life and had impregnated her in the back seat of his BMW outside Zum Zum, the trendy nightclub in the seventies, located in Buceo's small port, which gathered the young high bourgeoisie from Carrasco, Punta Gorda, and Pocitos. When Javier insisted years later on knowing his father's name and whereabouts, his mother told him he was the son of a foreigner, a "Bobby without a last name," as she described him. A mercenary with no fixed address, missing in action. When her son demanded more details, Carlota grabbed his arms, shaking him, and forbade him to speak of it again. She also intimidated the domestic staff not to bring up the topic.

The boy lived most of the time under Consuelo's tutelage in the Ferraro house while his mother flew around the world in first class or was admitted, vomiting, in upscale alcoholic clinics in the capital. Sofía always said that Consuelo cared for and educated that boy as if she had given birth to him. From an early age, the brat already looked strange, with black pupils, firm and implacable. "The grandfather's eyes," Consuelo Flores said.

"Thank you very much for coming, Consuelo. We barely got to talk at the funeral yesterday. What would you like to drink?" said Adrián as he sat down.

"No, nothing for me. Thank you, Mr. Adrián," said Consuelo, lowering her head with a humble smile.

"Forget the formalities. Call me Adrián, just Adrián. Come on, I'm buying. I don't like drinking alone."

"Well . . . a Coke with ice."

"And to eat?"

"Nothing, thank you. You know I have a small appetite."

"That's why you're always so slim, woman! Well, I'm going to have my second cappuccino, accompanied by two ham and cheese croissants. Maybe you'll feel like helping me with one, alright?" he said just as the waiter stood in front of the table.

"Well, alright, Mr. Adrián . . . I mean . . . Adrián," she corrected, smiling tightly and lowering her head again.

The Galician (as Uruguayans called all Spaniards), with a heavy accent from the motherland and slicked-back hair, took the order and shouted towards the counter: "Manolo, two Imperial croissants, a short cappuccino, and a Coke with ice!"

"And how's life treating you? Are you married or have a boyfriend?"

"No, my time has passed, Adrián," she replied, wrinkling her forehead with the resigned expression of an eighty-year-old. "I still follow the same routine. Taking care of children born from other wombs. Scrubbing other people's kitchens and bathrooms. When Mr. Ferraro was widowed, I kept taking care of him until he passed away. May that poor tormented soul rest in peace," she said serenely, with a distant look. The detective was momentarily surprised by the comment but quickly justified it as coming from someone who had deeply inhaled the public marital infidelities of the magnate who, upon reaching senility, might have ended up confessing the torturous memories of an unrestrained libido to his maid.

"Mrs. Carlota took me to her house in Carrasco until she moved to the penthouse in Punta Carretas. By then, she had hit hard times and soon told me she could no longer afford to have a live-in maid."

"And who cleaned the penthouse? She was useless for that kind of work."

"She cut my salary and asked me to come once a week for two or three hours."

"And what day did you go?"

"Sunday mornings at seven."

"So early? And who let you in? At that hour, the doorman was probably asleep," said Adrián, casually stroking his mustache.

"I had a key. When I arrived, she was still sleeping off the previous night's party. She wanted me to come early to clean up the mess from the Saturday night parties and drunkenness. Her friends left everything a mess," said the maid, twisting her mouth in disgust.

"When was the last time you saw her?"

"Two weeks before she was found dead."

"But didn't you go once a week?"

"Yes, but she decided to skip a Sunday and told me not to come the next. She sometimes did that if she went to Punta del Este or had other plans."

"And Javier? Does the brat ever call you?" Adrián said while smoothing his hair.

"No, sir . . . sorry . . . Adrián. Excuse me. What a silly head I have! It's hard for me to address you informally," she smiled, raising her eyebrows. "Young Javier lives nearby in his bachelor pad. Sometimes I see him around the neighborhood, but he acts like he doesn't see me."

"That little bastard! The same coldness as Carlota!"

"I don't take offense. He never had anyone to love him."

"But Consuelo! You raised him like a mother while Carlota skied with her lovers in Bariloche. You were the one who dressed him, combed his hair, helped him with his schoolwork while she traveled the world playing executive or detoxing in alcoholic clinics!"

The maid raised her eyebrows, closed her eyes, and nodded.

"Actually, the reason for this meeting was to ask you for Javier's address. Maybe he knows something about Carlota's recent activities," added the detective.

"Yesterday, after the funeral Sofía mentioned that you are investigating the case. I still can't believe you two aren't together anymore. You looked so happy before going to the United States. What an injustice of life!"

"No injustice, Consuelo. In this life, you reap what you sow, and I'm paying for my past mistakes. I didn't deserve Sofía. No drama . . . let's change the subject."

"If you want, I can accompany you to Javier's apartment. He has had very little contact with you, and perhaps seeing me will make it easier."

"Thank you, Consuelo, but I'd prefer to go alone," said Adrián just as the waiter arrived with breakfast. "Come on, give it a try; it looks good," he added, pushing a croissant towards her.

"Well, thank you, Mr. Adrián. Just so as not to be ungrateful," she said, hesitantly picking up the pastry with her fingertips.

"Look who's there," said Adrián, looking out the window towards the sidewalk across the street.

"Who?"

"Alonso, the doorman of Carlota's building. Don't you know him?" said Adrián, surprised, as he prepared to bite into the second croissant, overflowing with ham and cheese.

She turned her eyes to the table and said, "Only by sight."

Adrián watched her closely. It seemed strange to him that she hadn't recognized the doorman. She seemed to feel the weight of his gaze and lowered her eyes to avoid it but quickly clarified, "I'm a bit near-sighted. I didn't recognize him from afar."

Then, they changed the subject and rejoiced with old and funny stories of the Ferraro family. Not everything is drama, not even in hell.

# XI

THE BOY JAVIER, AS Consuelo still called him, or "the insolent brat," as Adrián labeled him, was already twenty years old. He lived on the fifth floor of a building located at Boulevard España and Rambla República del Perú. The detective went without notifying him. Otherwise, he wouldn't have seen him. It was eleven in the morning when he pressed the intercom button. He trusted he would find him because he calculated that he wouldn't wake up before that time. When he answered through the intercom, Adrián announced himself with a false name. He said he was a friend of his Aunt Sofía in the United States and that he brought him a gift from her. Javier asked how he knew his address. Adrián explained that Consuelo had provided it. The young man took the bait and let him in. When he stepped out the elevator, the door to the apartment was ajar. He knocked lightly with his knuckles.

"Come in," said the sleepy voice. Javier was lying on the couch with his legs propped up on the living room table. A marble ashtray overflowing with cigarette butts adorned it. The smell of marijuana was obvious. There were six empty Budweiser cans scattered on the carpet. He brushed back his straight, jet-black hair, which fell long on the sides, framing his runway-model features. He glared at the detective with the black, opaque, impenetrable pigment of his eyes, inherited from his mother and grandfather, reinforcing his disdain by keeping his generous, well-balanced eyebrows arched. His turned-up nose and full lips, like Elvis Presley's, rounded out an almost feminine beauty. Upon seeing Adrián, he jumped like a cat and exclaimed:

"Ah, the gold digger! Consuelo should have warned me it was you. Well . . . after all, one could never expect common sense from a servant. Behold, ladies and gentlemen," he said, raising his hand solemnly as if speaking to an imaginary audience, "another of the many predators who prowled around my aunt's or my mother's fortune! Anyway, I'm glad to know Sofía managed to get rid of you." He paused, raised his right eyebrow, and asked sideways, "So . . . which is the gift? (with a perfect English accent acquired at the British School). I suppose by now even people like you have learned a bit of the language of the North."

Adrián smiled as he approached the sofa.

"That shitty face has the Ferraro upbringing stamped on your forehead, 'little Javier,'" he said, while grabbing him by the hair and starting to drag him across the carpet. The young man opened his mouth wide, his gypsy eyes bulging from the unexpected maneuver. "Servant, the one who loved you more than your mother?" added Adrián, gritting his teeth as he continued dragging him among the beer cans. "Apologize, chicken, even if Consuelo isn't here or I'll send you to hell along with your mother!"

Javier whimpered like a pig in a slaughterhouse.

"Kneel and apologize, piece of shit, or you'll end up with dentures," insisted Adrián, pulling his hair that crunched between his fingers.

"Okay, okay! Sorry, sorry!" said Javier, crouching, trembling, stuttering. The detective loosened the grip on his hair and with a sharp, resounding slap on the back of his neck, ordered:

"Now, go sit down, you wretch. The gold digger is going to ask you some questions."

The young man complied, crawling on all fours towards the couch. Adrián sat in front of him, on the coffee table.

"Who frequented your mother's apartment, brat?"

"How should I know! The usual sycophants or a mafia Jew who introduced her as his girlfriend."

"Who, Stern?"

Javier studied his eyes. Then he said:

"Yes, that lowlife with whom my mother ended up after a lifetime of elegance! She had the nerve to say that disgusting fat man was the love of her life!"

"And the painting of the white wolf? Who has it hidden, you?"

Javier looked at him intently and then spat:

"Fuck you! I'm sick of your questions. Either you get lost, or you'll have to deal with the cops . . ." He didn't finish the sentence because Adrián had already thrown a punch that split his full lips. His mouth bled like a skinned rose. He let out a fragile, vulnerable cry, almost like a child.

"Don't hit me anymore, you animal! I don't know anything about that painting! Stern probably took it."

"What else do you know, you bastard, about the relationship with Stern?" said Adrián, stretching towards the couch to twist the neck of his pajamas. "He is married. Did he appear in public with your charming mother?"

"No, they spent most of the time in the chalet the Jew has in Punta del Este. His wife and kids only went there in the summer. The rest of the year, he used it with my mother."

"Where is the chalet located?"

"In Pinares, at stop 20."

"And you, how do you know so much about the chalet? Did you go there too?"

"I went surfing in Punta del Este and sometimes saw them, hugging on the promenade. My mother told me they were in Pinares and invited me to dinner with them, but I never went. I wasn't going to lower myself to step into the den of a lowlife. She made her choice if she decided to downgrade. Well . . . it ended badly for her. Most likely, that scum was the one who killed her."

Adrián loosened the pressure on the young man's neck and wiped the blood from his knuckles on the pajamas.

"That's all for now, pendejo. I'm leaving, assuming you didn't hide anything from me. May God have mercy on your filthy existence if I have to pay you another visit."

He lit a cigarette and threw the still-lit match on the young man's body. Javier shook and put it out with his hands. Adrián blew a puff of smoke in his face before standing up. Javier started coughing while wiping the sweat from his forehead with his sleeve. The detective smirked mockingly. Then he turned around, opened the door, and walked leisurely towards the elevator.

# XII

On Monday morning, Adrián headed towards Punta del Este. After driving for an hour and a half on the new road, he spotted the peninsula of the country's most famous resort town on the horizon, with its skyscrapers jutting into the Atlantic waters. The Pinares neighborhood had no apartment buildings. Municipal regulations only allowed for one or two-story residences. Particularly notable were the enormous thatched-roof chalets scattered along streets with crazy geometry, devoid of square blocks. The facades were dominated by brick walls either coated with lime or painted in aged ochre tones. He didn't know the address of "Cheeks" Stern. At that time of the morning, the resort was deserted of homeowners. He only saw gardeners maintaining the chalets year-round.

"Good morning, amigo. What a luxury this garden! It's clear you know what you're doing," he said to a good-natured looking man cutting the grass. The local offered a humble smile with the few teeth he had left.

"Thank you, we do what we can. This year the weather is cooperating. It's rained a lot, and the grass appreciates it."

The detective took out a cigar and offered one to the man, who accepted gladly. "I'm lost. I'm looking for Cheeks Stern's residence. Do you know him?"

"How could I not know him, my friend? He's more famous than the president," he said, smiling again. "Look, follow this street to the second corner, turn right on Sagitario, then take the first left on Tucán. Then go all the way to the end. The house is the last one on the culdesá."

Adrián assumed he meant Cul de Sac, as the wealthy Argentinians, always obsessed with foreign terminology, called dead-end streets.

"It's a thatched-roof house with a claret-colored front. You can't miss it," the man continued. Adrián thanked him with a handshake and headed to the place. The mansion was grandiose, enormous in proportions but lacking in good taste. He decided to wait until night. He went to the nearby city of Maldonado and parked in front of Las Carretas bar, located in the main square, where on his last visit to the resort he had delighted in a tripe stew. Autumn was coming with winter airs, and the day was ideal for putting something warm in his body. He took a nap in the car and stretched the remaining daylight by walking around the small port of Punta del Este. He sat on the same rock where he had embraced Sofía while watching the red disc hide in the sea. When dusk enveloped the resort, he returned to Pinares. He parked the car in the cul-de-sac, a few meters from the house. He sneaked between the pines of the neighboring chalet to avoid the surveillance cameras posted at the front of the residence. He jumped over the wooden fence and crawled across the lawn to the side wall, in case there were any other hidden cameras in the pines. No lights detecting his movements turned on, so he continued around the perimeter to the back window facing the pool. He saw the anti-theft alarm sensors on the doors and windows when he pointed the flashlight inside. He didn't want to enter. He wasn't an expert at deactivating electronic systems and wanted to leave as he had arrived. Without running. So, he decided to look through a circular window higher up on the facade. He deduced it was a bathroom by the tiles reflecting the flashlight's light. He couldn't reach it, so he grabbed some logs from the grill and stood on them. The flashlight revealed the monumental jacuzzi and all the other extravagances of a bathroom that had the dimensions of a tiny bachelor apartment in a modest neighborhood. Curiously, the door was open, revealing part of the bedroom. He increased the flashlight's intensity and focused on the wall against which the bed rested. His mouth opened, stunned. Above the headboard hung the painting of the white wolf. Striking, just as it had been imprinted on his retinas the first time, he had seen it hanging in the Ferraro residence. He felt elated. Like when he went fishing with his father and cast the line into the water without much expectation, and suddenly a silverside tugged at the rod. He couldn't believe it. He focused again. He scanned the painting along the edges and on the upper edge, the paint was still cracked and slightly peeling. There was no doubt. His senses were not deceiving him. "Cheeks" Stern had the painting of the white wolf in his Pinares residence. Why there and not in Montevideo? To hide it from curious minds, or was there another reason? He returned to the car with the smile of a child who finds a hidden treasure under a stone. The neighborhood remained quiet, but just in case, he turned the ignition key and gently pressed the accelerator. He drove away slowly in second gear. He didn't want to tempt his good luck too much.

# XIII

EVEN THOUGH THE NEXT day was a workday, El Yoruga bar was overflowing with people having dinner at 10 PM. Many young couples were savoring the classic and popular Chivito, accompanied by a mountain of fries and Pilsen beer, the national brand. Adrián was leaning back, balancing on the rear legs of his chair, admiring the microscopic miniskirt of a stunning brunette.

"See if you can get me an interview with Bermúdez," he said to "Rabbit" Vergara, who was making a little boat out of a paper napkin while they waited for two whiskeys and a platter of sausage and cheese.

"Don't ask me for weird things, Adrián. He won't see you. You know very well that the police don't like private detectives, and even less in your case."

"Why less in my case?"

"Obviously. You come from the United States. You're not as easy to bribe as the locals to get you to stop bothering and asking questions. Do you understand?" said Rabbit with a superior look.

"Without a doubt, he's just as easy to bribe as all the cops. I'll send him a bottle of Scotch and that's it!"

"Get that out of your head, Adrián. If I see an opportunity, I'll arrange it, but I bet he won't want to. Well, here comes the whiskey!" exclaimed Rabbit, rubbing his hands enthusiastically, showing his exuberant teeth.

The rest of the conversation fell on more trivial matters. They reminisced about their time as students at high school number 17. Rabbit twisted with his shameless laughter, attracting the glances of other tables. While his friend laughed, Adrián looked through the window at the Peugeot 504 parked on the sidewalk across the street. The driver had turned off the lights and remained inside. Adrián assumed he was waiting for someone.

"What do you call a dog with a fever?" asked Rabbit.

Adrián said nothing. He just stared at him, waiting for the punchline.

"Hot dog!" said Rabbit, bursting into laughter.

"Come on, call the waiter, clown. Let's pay up, I have to get up early tomorrow."

As they left, they said goodbye with a hug and went in opposite directions. The detective noticed that the Peugeot was still parked across the street. Besides the driver, there was someone sitting in the back seat. The tinted windows didn't let him distinguish their faces. Only the glow of the cigarettes gave away their presence. He started walking towards the hotel. The street was deserted. It was almost midnight. Suddenly, he saw three individuals crossing the road at a rapid pace. He knew they were coming for him. The first one to arrive threw a punch at his face. He dodged it. His reflexes were still in good shape thanks to the boxing training of his teenage years. He unleashed a powerful right hook that landed squarely on the attacker's chin. The man staggered and collapsed on the sidewalk like a marionette with its strings cut. Adrián turned left to face the second attacker. It was too late to dodge the punch.

"Here you go, bastard! To help with your digestion," said another man with a thick mustache that almost covered his mouth but where, despite the dim light, a gold tooth could be seen. Still on his feet but doubled over in a fetal position, Adrián gasped for air. He tasted the sweet flavor of blood escaping from the corner of his lips. A second punch to the back of the head finished him off, and he fell to his knees on the sidewalk. He grimaced in pain. He felt darkness closing in. He struggled to open his eyes and managed to see the shiny loafers of a third man approaching.

"So, you're tough and hit young guys . . ." said the one with the shiny shoes. He paused briefly. He threw away the cigarette hanging from his mouth and swung his right leg in the air. Then he kicked Adrián in the head with the passion of someone taking a penalty kick in the World Cup. Adrián sensed the move and managed to shield himself with his arms. He rolled onto his left side. The one who had fallen like a puppet was already back on his feet. He followed his accomplice's example and landed another kick to the detective's ribs while saying to the others:

"He broke my jaw! I'll kill this son of a bitch, Daniel!"

"Calm down, Whispers! We're only supposed to mess up his face."

Adrián clung to Whispers' leg. He bit his calf with the fervor of a rabid dog. The big guy howled like a pig in the slaughterhouse. The other two, who had lagged, returned to the attack. At that moment, a car sped onto the sidewalk, and its headlights blinded Adrián and his assailants. The detective heard the screech of brakes followed by a dull, solid thud. He squinted more to see better. A figure crossed through the air in slow motion, thrown by the impact.

"Son of a bitch!" shouted the one called Daniel, seeing the mustached man with the gold tooth crash against the corner wall. Whispers stared, disoriented, at the car's headlights. Adrián saw the lion emblem. It was a Peugeot. The rear door opened, and Lucrecia's shaved head poked out, shouting hoarsely:

"Come on, tough guy, get in, I don't have all night!"

He crawled on all fours toward the vehicle as Lucrecia pulled him by his shirt.

"Let's go, Juana!" ordered the art dealer to the driver. With determination and skill, the woman behind the wheel shifted into reverse. The car screeched again and spun in a semicircle. Then Juana shifted into first gear and floored it, zooming away from the confused thugs.

"Well, tough guy, you were born again tonight," said Lucrecia with her typical laugh as they drove down the boulevard. The same self-satisfied laugh Adrián remembered very well from his first visit to her apartment at the Palacio Salvo.

"And now, where are we going?" asked Juana's shadow, with a square head and broad trucker shoulders.

"Home, woman. To nurse the baby's wounds," replied Lucrecia, stroking the detective's head.

# XIV

SEEN FROM PLAZA INDEPENDENCIA at midnight, the imposing bulk of the Palacio Salvo was a shadowy mass almost blending into the night. The exception was the large window on the seventeenth floor where a soft, manila-colored light escaped from Lucrecia's living room, barely outlining the heads of the gargoyles guarding the balcony of the One-armed Woman. Cold compresses were restoring circulation. Lucrecia's driver delicately calculated the pressure her big hands applied to the wounds. Adrián lay stretched out on the living room sofa. His cheekbones were swollen, his eyes blackened, and he felt a numbing sensation in his mouth. He couldn't feel his lips. While Juana treated him, her mistress prepared some drinks at the bar.

"Here, take this," Lucrecia said, handing him a well-loaded glass of Johnny Walker. "Let's see if your black label friend soothes your wounds, handsome."

Adrián drank eagerly until the glass was half empty and then lay back down, submissive to Juana's treatment, who insisted on the cold cloth. Sometimes, the driver would take a break and take a drag from the cigarette she had left resting in the ashtray.

"My instinct told me that Peugeot wasn't parked there by chance," the detective commented. "Why were you following me? Should I report you to the authorities for sexual harassment?"

Lucrecia let out her usual loud laugh as she opened the windows a third of the way to let in the slight sea breeze.

"Nothing like that, chick. Just watching your back, hahaha! Although I see you know how to defend yourself very well."

"Damn, I never thought I'd awaken your maternal instinct," he said, frowning at the pressure Juana now applied with another compress on his ribs.

"Maternal instinct, my ass! We have common interests, detective. I want to know where the white wolf painting ended up, and my instinct tells me you might be on the trail. Besides, Carlota was one of my unsatisfied carnal crushes, hahaha. Despite my persistent advances, I could never overcome her prejudice. She'll never know what she missed, hehe."

"She never seemed very prejudiced to me."

"Maybe I was wrong, and she really was heterosexual, the bitch," she said with another vigorous laugh. Then she adopted a more formal expression. "Seriously, I tell you I'd love for us to find the killer. I'm sure it was Bonilla, and he also has the painting. When the poor Carlota heard his name, her blood froze. If that dictator bastard killed her, I want to be the first to know. I'm betting on you and not the police investigation," she finished seriously, pointing at him with her finger. "Otherwise, after a few weeks, the file will end up at the bottom of a drawer in Commissioner Bermúdez's office."

"If it was Bonilla, I'll volunteer to finish off that bastard," interrupted the driver, punching the glass table, making the cigarette butts jump out of the ashtray.

"That's an extra reason for us to be partners, handsome," said Lucrecia, noticing the surprised reaction on Adrián's face at Juana's comment. "Juana belongs to the group of relatives of the disappeared during the dictatorship. They've been after evidence that could convict Bonilla for the disappearances of political prisoners. There are well-founded rumors that the bastard liked to film the torture sessions. That would be compelling to prosecute him. I'm trying to help them."

"Congratulations, Marchand. I see you've become quite the bulwark in the service of good causes."

The one-armed Woman laughed again, but this time not so loudly.

"It happens, handsome, that during my years in the Middle East, interviewing every dictator bastard born in those lands, I developed a special rash for that type of vermin. If I can do something for my local friends, I still have a hand to offer."

"Don't go on, you'll make me cry," said Adrián with a mocking smile as he stretched his right leg on the sofa to relax his muscles. Then he did the same with the left.

Lucrecia gave him a piercing look, and he knew how to read body language to realize when he had crossed the line.

"Relax, it's a joke, woman!"

"Besides, we could kill two birds with one stone," she continued, playing with an ice cube in her mouth, trying to hide that she wasn't the iceberg she usually advertised.

"How so?"

"Carlota had been the lover of the military man right at the time of the dictatorship. Maybe she knew something about that tape. What if that was the motive for the crime, huh?"

"Those who attacked Adrián were Bonilla's men," interrupted Juana. "I've seen them leave his residence in Prado more than once."

"But how did Bonilla find out so quickly that our detective is investigating Carlota's murder?" Lucrecia wondered, biting her lower lip.

"It was Javier who tipped them off," said Adrián.

"Carlota's son?" Lucrecia exclaimed, widening her eyes.

"The very same. I was at his apartment twisting his neck, and he turned to his mother's former lover to teach me a lesson. I should have hit him harder."

"Could he be the one who has the white wolf painting? We should sneak into his apartment to see if he has it hidden there," said Lucrecia.

Adrián wrinkled his nose and brow, shaking his head.

"So, what's the next step, partner?" insisted the one-armed woman, seeing that he disapproved of her idea.

Adrián smiled and promised to call her the next day. He didn't want to offend her. Despite being grateful to the Spaniard for saving his skin, he wasn't too keen on having her as a partner. Lucrecia was still on his list of suspects, especially because of her noticeable interest and insistence in knowing the whereabouts of the white wolf painting. However, Stern had the painting. Had he beaten Lucrecia to it?

This reasoning didn't fully convince him either. It was a very valuable painting, but did it justify such a ruthless crime? Stern already had an enormous fortune. Did Lucrecia and Stern know each other? He wouldn't ask the one-armed woman just yet. She was very astute, and he didn't intend to alert her to his thoughts.

# XV

It had been years since Adrián had stopped at the
corner of San José and Yi streets, where the Montevideo police headquarters was located. The building
occupied half a block along the two streets. Its facade
was a dull gray Art Deco, the ideal color to symbolize
the existential flatness within. He had no fond memories of the place. The central jail was also there, where
he had spent twenty-four hours in his youth after a
drunken brawl at a boîte. The second visit was during
the dictatorship. He and Rabbit Vergara had gone to
rescue a neighborhood friend from the clutches of a
sergeant named Soria. They knew the officer liked to
use electric shocks on students who had made the mis-

take of joining the Communist Party, even if they had never engaged in any seditious activity. His friend was one of those idealists, and they weren't about to let the sergeant fry his balls. He still remembered Soria's foul breath, reeking of cheap alcohol, when he received them in the visiting room. Spitting as he spoke, Soria had informed them that he didn't think the suspect would be released that day.

"Well, I'm not leaving until I go with him," Adrián had said.

"What did you say?" the officer reacted, with fierce eyes, bringing his breath and sweat closer to Adrián's face.

"I'm not leaving until you stop tickling his balls! He's a useless fool who did nothing more than have a stupid membership card with the leftists."

"Rabbit" Vergara, who even then was better than Adrián at dealing with the corrupt, interrupted the confrontation.

"Hold on, tin kettle, let me handle this," he whispered to his friend. "Listen, Soria, I'm the son of Commissioner Vergara," he said immediately, addressing the sergeant in a conciliatory tone. "Do I have to talk to my father to resolve this matter? I don't want to bother him with trivialities, but if there's no other choice . . ."

Soria widened his egg-like eyes and then squinted them. Rabbit held his gaze. Then the sergeant changed his tune and smiled while pulling out a handkerchief to wipe the profuse sweat dripping from his two-day-old beard and collecting in the folds of his double chin. He almost had no neck, as if his head had been nailed to his shoulders.

"If you want to wait, go ahead and wait, but I have no idea when he'll be released," he had said.

They didn't have to stand by more than forty-five minutes. Commissioner Vergara's name was already legendary among the officers of the time. That had been one of the many times Rabbit Vergara had gotten Adrián out of trouble. The detective smiled at the memory.

Now, here he was again, entering the club of uniformed men with a license to commit crimes. It was about Sofía, he told himself, and she was worth the effort.

"I've come to see Commissioner Bermúdez," he told the female officer at the front desk.

"Do you have an appointment?"

"No but tell him I have very important information about the murder of Carlota Ferraro."

The woman turned and went through a door with frosted glass at the back of the counter. She reappeared a few minutes later and motioned with her finger for him to follow. They walked through a dark, window-less corridor to the elevator. They went up to the sec-ond floor, and the officer knocked on a door marked "Commissioner's Office."

"Come in," said a muffled, hoarse voice. The hier-arch was sitting with his feet on the desk, talking on the phone. On his right there was a portrait of a seven or eight-year-old girl, Adrián estimated, bearing the same unattractive genes as the man in front of him.

"Alright, keep me posted," he said to end the call, hanging up the receiver. "What can I do for you, my friend?" he added seriously and formally as he stood to extend his hand. He was wearing a navy-blue suit with an untied tie. He wasn't tall but was stocky, and his large hands seemed made for crushing, but he shook hands limply, as toadies usually do. His restless brown pupils moved quickly, scanning the detective's entire body.

"Have a seat," Bermúdez said as he swatted a fly that coveted the sweat on his forehead. To the left of the desk was an old standing fan that squeaked like a rattletrap but failed to alleviate the sticky air in the office.

"My name is Adrián Fontana. I live in the United States. I'm a private detective hired by the victim's sister to assist in the investigation."

Bermúdez looked at him seriously for four or five seconds. Then he flashed a cynical smile.

"To assist us? But . . . do we look like we need foreign help to solve a local homicide? Look, my friend, I don't have time to spare, and you didn't even make an appointment," he said, drumming his fingers on the desk. "They tell me you have important information. What do you know?" he added impatiently, raising his chin before reclining back in his swivel chair.

"Truthfully, nothing specific yet, but I must be close to something hot because last night Lieutenant Colonel Yamandú Bonilla set his dogs on me to rearrange my face. Do you know him?" Adrián said, now studying the body language.

The commissioner showed a nervous tic in his left eye but quickly recovered. He adjusted himself in his seat. The persistent fly landed on his face again. He swatted it away angrily. He loosened his tie a bit more.

"Of course. Who doesn't know Bonilla, but . . . that's a very serious accusation. Do you have proof?" he said, slowly rolling up a magazine with Maradona's face on the cover.

"All in due time, Bermúdez," Adrián replied as he lit a cigarette. He took a deep drag and exhaled the smoke to the side. "By the way, have you determined if the victim had any paintings stolen from her art collection? One in particular disappeared from her apartment."

Bermúdez's arm shot out to the desk, crushing the insolent fly with the magazine.

"Mr. Fontana, we cannot share the progress of the official investigation with you. I don't know what painting you're talking about, and now if you'll excuse me . . ." he said, standing to indicate the end of the conversation.

Adrián threw another dart:

"Maybe 'Cheeks' Stern knows something. He was Carlota's last lover. Have you questioned him?"

The commissioner closed his eyes, took a deep breath, held it for a moment, and then deflated like a yoga exercise.

"As I said, Fontana, we don't share investigation details with private detectives, especially those from

Yankee country. Did you see what just happened to the fly for poking its nose where it wasn't called?"

"I get it, Bermúdez, I get it. Have a good day," Adrián said as he stood. He winked and flashed a mocking smile while giving a slow military salute, touching his right hand to his temple. Then, he slowly turned toward the door.

"Do you know what my mom used to tell me when we went to the beach?" Bermúdez insisted. "Son, go slow on the rocks. Be careful, Fontana. Don't slip on the moss. It's friendly advice. Don't get into trouble. Leave it to us; sooner or later, we'll catch the culprit."

Adrián smiled sideways and left the office. The whole conversation hadn't lasted more than a few minutes, but the goal was to meet Bermúdez. He achieved his aim: to irritate him. Now he had to wait for the reaction. To see which way the waters stirred. He knew he was playing with fire, but the memory of Sofía crying in his office increased his courage and adrenaline. As he stepped out onto the street, he lit a Nevada, checked the time, and saw it was eleven in the morning. He headed to the Mercado del Puerto. He had a meeting with "Rabbit" Vergara. While driving, he thought about all the connecting points. "Cheeks"

Stern was the godfather of the commissioner's daughter in charge of the investigation. That alone was a farce that stripped any hint of seriousness from the official inquiry. On the other hand, Lieutenant Colonel Bonilla, Carlota's former lover during the dictatorship, maintained some macabre connection with Javier. Undoubtedly, Sofía was right. By tempting the devil too much, getting involved with the most twisted characters on the Montevideo scene, her sister had likely ended up cooked in her own sauce.

# XVI

Whenever Adrián traveled to Montevideo, the Mercado del Puerto was a mandatory stop. Built in the 19th century when metallic architecture on iron bases was still an unknown process in America, it gained fame when Eiffel erected his tower in Paris. The structure had been manufactured in England and was now over a century old. Originally intended to supply meat, fruits, and vegetables to the ships docking at Montevideo's port, it eventually became the city's most vital gastronomic hub. Celebrities like Carlos Gardel and Enrico Caruso had strolled through its internal streets. Flanking the entrance were the most elegant and expensive restaurants: El Palenque and

La Posada del Puerto, which attracted the families of cruise ship travelers. But the interesting part, the bohemia, the idiosyncrasy of the Río de la Plata, was inside. The venue was perhaps Montevideo's most fascinating sociological experiment. Sitting on the stools or standing at the bar were the most diverse representatives of Uruguayan society. It wasn't uncommon to be having a drink next to a politician, an ambassador, a gangster, or a pimp. All anesthetized, separated from their castes for a while, united in a delirious ritual of alcohol, tobacco, and carnivorous diet. In the old days, Adrián loved to roam the bars and recognize friends among a thousand virile voices all speaking at the same time, creating a high-decibel murmur that only diminished if one chose to sit at La Planchita de Alejandro, an intimate corner, farther from the central corridor. Now he barely recognized anyone. As soon as he passed through the huge wrought iron gate, the aroma of meat impregnated with coronilla smoke and the sizzle of melted fat reviving the embers made his mouth water. A cloud of burnt wood escaped through the high chimneys, zigzagged for a while among the Victorian beams, then fled through the extractors toward the port promenade, flirting with the senses of motorists passing with their windows open. Sun-beams pierced the crust of the stained-glass windows on the ceiling and landed on the flagstone floor or the heads of the patrons.

He amused himself for a moment, watching tourists hypnotized by the grills the size of a one-and-a-half-bed, displaying all kinds of beef, lamb, pork, and offal cuts. There was also grilled hake, cod, or cheese. What caught the foreigners' attention the most were the chinchulines, sweetbreads, kidneys, and sweet or savory blood sausages. When the grill masters explained that chinchulín is the cow's intestine, they made a face of disgust that quickly changed to one of satisfaction when they tried it accompanied by the classic chimichurri. The same happened when they learned that blood sausage is made with pig's blood. Caution at first and delight in the end. The past rushed through the detective's mind. The New Year's toast, the end-of-course celebration, the drunken brawls, the February carnival, or any other excuse to go celebrate with friends. He remembered when he and Sofía would go on Saturdays at noon. He was absent for a few seconds. "We shouldn't have left," he murmured to himself. He wondered if the voluntary exile they had embarked on had split their tribal identity in two. With half their body in the north and the other half in the south. Was this what separated him from Sofía? But then he reacted. "Don't fool yourself, Fontana. It's not a matter of geography. The problem is you!"

Adrián sat at the corner of Roldós' bar to wait for "Rabbit" Vergara. To start off, he ordered a bottle of medio y medio, two glasses, and a sandwich with turkey filling. He was taking a bite when he felt a pat on the back.

"Well-chilled medio y medio! You know what's good, old man, hahaha!" said Rabbit. Adrián filled the other glass and raised his hand to the waiter.

"A carrot for my friend, please." The waiter looked puzzled, as if trying to figure out if he had heard correctly.

"Screw you, idiot! Don't listen to this clown, sir. Bring me a sandwich with black bread and mondiola, please," said Rabbit. Then he laughed and raised his glass.

"Cheers, brother, for the reunion!"

"Cheers, Vergara."

"And that bruise on your eye?"

"A little souvenir from Bonilla's men. Last night, after we said goodbye at El Yoruga."

Rabbit was left with his mouth open for a few seconds. Then he said:

"But how did they spot you so quickly? How did Bonilla find out about you?"

Adrián explained that after slapping Javier, he probably ran to Bonilla to teach him a lesson.

"Damn, man! So, the kid also has a thing for uniforms, just like his mother."

"Did you hear anything about how 'Cheeks' Stern's relationship with Carlota was?" Adrián asked as he took another bite of his turkey sandwich.

"The truth is, Adrián, everyone agrees on the same thing," said Rabbit, raising his eyebrows, shrugging, and shaking his head as if about to announce an irrefutable diagnosis. "They were very much in love. According to his friends, Cheeks always said, 'this woman moved my world.' They told me that when one of his men, "Flea" Sarmiento, brought him the news of the murder, he punched him. They say he was hitting him while crying inconsolably. But . . ." Rabbit suddenly stopped. He furrowed his brow and squinted his eyes. "Why do you look so incredulous? Can't a man fall in love? I don't think he had anything to do with the crime."

"Maybe, Vergara, but the fact is that he apparently was also in love with Carlota's paintings. One of her most valuable artworks is hanging in Cheeks's mansion in Punta del Este."

"And how do you know that, Adrián?"

"I saw it with my own eyes. The other night I sneaked into his house in Pinares. He has the painting hanging in his bedroom."

"Did I hear right? You went to Punta del Este and broke into Cheeks's house?" said Rabbit, narrowing his eyes and wrinkling his nose as if he smelled something foul. Immediately, his face turned red, and he started blinking as if suffering from a nervous disorder.

"Well . . . not inside the house, I just peeked through a back window," Adrián said with a "not me" look on his face.

"Oh, no! You're a damn kamikaze!" Rabbit shouted; his face as red as the embers burning on the grill. He stood up on the stool, making hysterical gestures with his hands and gritting his teeth as if on the verge of an epileptic fit. Next to them, an old man sipping a beer froze with the edge of the mug on his lips. Rabbit usually didn't pay attention to the volume of his voice in public. This time he seemed aware of his surroundings. He saw the old man petrified with fear. He tried to compose himself. He took a deep breath and let it out all at once, then sat back down. He lowered his head and paused briefly. Then he stretched his long torso towards the detective, isolating the old man and the other patrons lined up at the bar with his back. He brought his face close to his friend's and whispered in his ear, "If Cheeks finds out, not only will he twist your balls but mine too! Are you fucking crazy?" He leaned back again, angry. "You don't mess with that beast! If they see me with you, I'm dead."

Adrián pressed his lips, trying to hide the amusement caused by seeing his friend gesticulating as if he had been told the world was ending. He couldn't hold back and burst out laughing. The old man next to them resumed drinking but still cautiously, considering the giant who had just erupted beside him.

"What are you laughing at, idiot?" said Rabbit, with his shoulders hunched, hands on his hips with his thumbs sticking backward and his elbows outward, perplexed that his obtuse friend was so unaware of the danger.

"Don't you think it's odd that Cheeks has the painting?" Adrián said, now serious, after regaining control of his laughter, while hanging a cigarette between his lips.

"And what do I know, man! Maybe she was so in love that she gave it to him."

"I doubt it, Vergara. Carlota didn't mix bedroom feelings with material possessions," Adrián replied, lighting the Nevada.

"Well, I don't know why the painting is there, and frankly, I don't care!" said Rabbit, downing his medio y medio and filling the glass again. "I told you, Adrián, that Cheeks is a rabid dog, and the first thing you do is go to Punta del Este without consulting me. You're fucking crazy! We're going to end up in a ditch with a bullet in the back of our heads!" he predicted, pointing at Adrián with an elevated finger and a mix of fear and anger in his eyes. He was so agitated that he turned to his plate and almost swallowed the mondiola sandwich in one bite. Adrián had to press his lips to hold back another burst of laughter.

"Calm down, brother. If Cheeks associates you with me, tell him we're school friends and that I'm investigating the crime. Explain that I knew they were lovers and that I must have found out about the Pinares house from another source, which is actually true. That you even tried to convince me he's not the killer. In short, Vergara, you have plenty of tricks to sound convincing."

"I don't like this at all, man!" said Rabbit, shaking his head compulsively, still chewing the three-quarters of the sandwich in his mouth.

Down the central aisle advanced a nearly naked brunette showgirl shaking her breasts and hips, followed by a small carnival troupe composed of four drummers frenetically beating their drums. Next to them, another group member extended a hat to the patrons, collecting tips. When they passed in front of Roldós, the detective turned on his stool and leaned his back against the bar to check out the butt of the brunette wearing a thong that almost disappeared between her buttocks. Meanwhile, Rabbit Vergara watched, possessed, as the juice of a round sausage made the embers sizzle.

"Hey, boss, can you give me half of that sausage and a whisky, please?" he said to the grill master. "Damn you, Adrián! You make me nervous, and the anxiety wakes up my appetite!"

Outside, the midday sun was already starting to heat the cobblestones. The siren of a cargo ship entering the port snapped Adrián out of his erotic fantasy. He turned back to his seat and pointed to the grill.

"And for me, please cut a portion of that ribeye that's been eyeing me for a while. Is it juicy?"

The grill master cut it in half and brought a piece to the bar on a fork.

"Do you like it like this?"

"Perfect, boss. Also, prepare a tomato salad with oil and oregano to go with this delicacy. Rabbit, will you join me with a red wine?"

"Rabbit" Vergara nodded while chewing.

"Bring us a Tannat from Garzón Wineries, please," Adrián said while cutting a piece of meat that barely offered any resistance to the knife.

"And if Cheeks asks me why I didn't tell him anything? Do you think that beast is an idiot?" said Rabbit.

"Damn, man. How do I have to spell it out for you? You warned me not to mess with him and thought you had convinced me. You blame it on me, Vergara. Stop overthinking it and enjoy the food with those beautiful incisors God gave you!" the detective concluded, messing up his friend's quiff.

"Rabbit" Vergara kept shaking his head like a pendulum, resisting his friend's logic. Adrián was glad he hadn't told him he had also gone to provoke Commissioner Bermúdez. It would have given him a heart attack, he thought. He focused back on the ribeye. He took a slice of bread, dipped it in the juice spread across the plate, and eagerly brought it to his mouth.

# XVII

ADRIÁN HAD DECIDED TO take the bull by the horns and pay a surprise visit to "Cheeks" Stern. He didn't know where to find him and asking "Rabbit" Vergara was not an option. His friend was already scared enough without adding more fuel to the fire. Whenever he visited Montevideo, he would drop by the L'Avenir club to greet his old and beloved boxing coach from his teenage years. He knew that Stern, apart from his passion for horse racing, also liked to promote up-and-coming boxers, and perhaps the old coach could help him find him. When he went down to the hotel lobby, the receptionist gave him her usual telepathic look of "Let's go to bed!" He acknowledged it and approached the counter.

"Any messages for me?"

"No, nothing has arrived, Mr. Fontana."

"Okay, thanks. You can call me Adrián," he said, arching an eyebrow and narrowing his eyes at the girl.

"Alright, místerAdrián," she said while undressing him with her eyes.

"Just Adrián. No need to be so formal. We're almost the same age."

The receptionist let out a sarcastic giggle and then said, "Then, I must have misread the date on your passport when I noted it in the guest file."

"Errors in the birth certificate records. I never bothered to correct them. I hate bureaucratic procedures," he said, continuing the game. "And how do you ask the hotel receptionist out for a drink without being told she doesn't mix work with pleasure?"

"Well, you just ask. Maybe today is your lucky day," said the cheeky brunette, skipping the hotel's professional conduct rules.

She looked about twenty-five years old. Her name was Graciela, and it was clear to Adrián that she was street-smart. They agreed to meet that night at the Bar

Anticuario, a popular spot in the Palermo neighborhood. He decided that the morning was perfect for a walk. He walked to the club, cutting through Punta Carretas to shorten the route along the promenade. The moderate caress of the autumn sun illuminated the neighborhood sidewalks. He smiled inwardly at the quintessential Montevideo scene of housewives burning little piles of dry leaves against the curb. It reminded him how different the world was where he had lived in recent years. In the United States, those small bonfires would have caused panic among the locals and immediately brought the fire department sirens. But in Montevideo, nothing. The women burned the autumn waste without anyone batting an eye. The wind pushed the foamy waves against the granite wall of the promenade. He thought of Sofía and the many walks they had taken together, arm in arm along the Río de la Plata. When he reached Parque Rodó, on the rocks of Ramírez Beach, a poorly dressed young fisherman with an adult face was trying to unhook a croaker that was still gasping its dying breaths on dry land. He continued towards Barrio Sur. He crossed the promenade, went up Paraguay Street, and turned right on Maldonado Street, where halfway down the block stood the club, its façade unchanged over time. The plaster stubbornly remained its usual dull gray, peeling and green with moisture where it met the sidewalk.

L'Avenir, located between the Palermo and Ciudad Vieja neighborhoods, was the oldest athletic institution in the country. It had been founded by French immigrants to cultivate the sporting spirit among the youth of the late nineteenth century. Its main activities were fencing, athletics, and boxing. Many renowned boxers from both sides of the Río de la Plata had trained in its ring, as well as politicians like Jorge Pacheco Areco, who became the president of the republic. The old Aimar Garmendia had trained most of the young people entering the sports institution for forty years, eager to start boxing. His pupils called him "the Basque" and respected him more than their parents. He was a man of few words and didn't often give compliments, but if he did, the boys' eyes would light up. After three months of convalescence due to a triple bypass surgery, he had returned to entertain himself by watching the training. He was around eighty years old and retired from the profession but still spent most of his day at the club he loved.

He remained faithful to his habit of holding the thermos under his right arm, clutching the leather-covered mate in the same hand while stirring the straw with his left. He poured himself a bitter "mate" while watching his successor, the dark-skinned Tulio Cuevas, explain the warm-up to the novices. The old man saw the detective coming down the stairs. The dull gray of his pupils lit up with enthusiasm. He put down the thermos and mate, rested his hands on his knees to stand up, tugged at his pants that had ridden up his backside, and advanced with difficulty.

They hugged, both struggling to hold back tears. The Basque stared at him, absorbed for a moment. Adrián did too. He still remembered the conversation he overheard by chance while peeing in the locker room.

"Who's that kid hitting the bag with so much anger?" the treasurer had asked the Basque. It was many years ago, but Adrián still remembered.

"His name is Adrián," the Basque had replied. "The kid is only fifteen but shows a lot of promise. He recently joined. He's been hitting hard from day one. Well, better he releases here than doing something stupid on the street."

"Why?"

"He's hitting at life."

Adrián looked at himself in the mirror. He squeezed a damn pimple from the acne that plagued his forehead. Then he approached the slightly open door to hear better. He watched them through the crack.

"Did something happen to him, Basque?" the treasurer had asked while picking his teeth with a toothpick.

"As they say, a year ago, his father abandoned him and his mother," the Basque said. "He went to Australia with a girl who could be his daughter."

"He's not the first nor the last!" the other had commented, cleaning the toothpick on the side of his pants and putting it in his shirt pocket.

"They were like two peas in a pod, but when he got infatuated with the girl, he forgot everything and took off."

"Poor kid, man! Hasn't he seen him since?"

"A year later, his father sent him a ticket, but the boy tore it up. He stayed with his mother."

"A good-hearted kid!" the treasurer had said.

There was a long pause. Adrián remembered how his coach had taken a long sip from the straw.

"That's right. He never talks about his father," the Basque had said more quietly, but Adrián could hear every word. Forty years had passed, and he seemed to remember them one by one. "Recently, he was suspended from school. A classmate taunted him about it. The joke cost the other kid his teeth."

Adrián returned to the ring to hit the bag with all the rage he had stored up.

"A tin pot. He heats up quickly!" the treasurer had commented as he rushed back to his office to answer the phone.

"Go on, kid, let it out . . . let it out!" Adrián looked at the sandbag and seemed to hear Aimar's demanding voice. He returned to the present when the Basque caressed his cheek with his arthritic hand.

"What's up, kid! Back in town again?" exclaimed the octogenarian with a raspy, lazy voice.

"That's right, Basque. So many new faces!"

"Yes, a bunch of still-green kids. The membership promotion is quite a success."

"I heard you had surgery, Basque," said Adrián, putting a hand on his shoulder.

"Yes, quite the cut. Want to see?" said the old man as he struggled to unbutton his shirt.

"Damn, what a big cut!"

"They opened me up like a grilled chicken, those bastards."

"And the cigarette, Basque?" said Adrián, seeing the pack in the guayabera pocket.

"Very well, thank you."

"He's not thinking of quitting, this shameless old man," interrupted Calixto, the cleaner, who was passing by with a bucket and brush in hand towards the locker rooms.

"Tomorrow. I'll start tomorrow," said the Basque. He paused, took out a cigarette, and observed it for a few seconds. Then he placed it behind his ear.

"But still always here, holding the fort. Tough old man!" said Adrián, changing the subject. Why try to spoil the old gladiator's small pleasures, he thought. Let him keep living and dying on his terms.

"Yes, I always come by for a while. They still ask me for advice sometimes, and I get bored in the tenement. The wife's not there anymore, rest her soul. What can I do between four walls? Here they always welcome me warmly and even give me something for dinner from what's left in the canteen. And you, what are you doing around here, still single?"

"Yes, Basque, still."

"And that pretty girl you introduced to me when you were going to the United States?"

"She's still pretty, Basque, but she has another man now."

"What a shame, you two seemed so happy! What happened, boy? Who misbehaved, you or her?" inquired the old man, with a mischievous smile that revealed the few teeth he had left.

"I did, Basque. It was me. She was and still is faithful. Let's change the subject, old man. I don't like to dwell on wounds. The past is past!" he said, feigning a low blow to the liver, while smiling and winking at him. "I came to greet you and ask you something you might know."

"Tell me, boy."

"I'm looking for 'Cheeks' Stern, where he lives or what bar he hangs out at. I remembered he liked to sponsor young boxers. Does he come around here?"

The old man studied his eyes. Then he said, "Cheeks Stern . . . I suppose you know he's a bad character. It's none of my business, and I don't ask what I'm not told, but whatever involves you with that pest, be careful. No, he doesn't come here, but I know he hangs out at the Palermo Boxing Club's canteen. He's training a guy from Paysandú, El Pollo Loco, who shows a lot of promise in the featherweight category. Go at night, around nine. He'll probably be there, surrounded by his cronies."

"And you don't know where he lives, here in Montevideo?"

"I think in Punta Gorda, near La Plaza de la Armada, but I'm not sure. Sometimes my wires get crossed, you know. It's the years, boy."

"Don't kid me, Basque! You can still take on quite a few," said Adrián, patting his shoulder. They stayed talking about old times. Sometimes Adrián would make a joke, and the old man would laugh heartily, choking on phlegm. Then they said goodbye with a bear hug that loosened as they resorted to patting each other's backs. Adrián knew that in some way, the Basque had replaced the father figure when he needed it most. Now he seemed so small, defenseless in his arms. He, who in his youth had seen him as so enormous, so omnipotent and indestructible. Even the quebracho trunk softens with the lashes of time.

# XVIII

"I HAVE WHAT YOU asked for," said "Rabbit" Vergara on the other end of the line. "The driver of the one-armed woman has a criminal record. You've got a good nose, Fontana."

Adrián, who had just stepped out of the shower, put his phone on speaker as he finished drying his hair.

"Good job, Rabbit! What else did you find out?"

"It turns out that three years ago, Juana was in a relationship with a woman from the Capurro neighborhood, who was married to a guy named Cardozo, much older than her. It seems the guy used to come home drunk and beat her up. One day, Zulema, that's the woman's name, showed up to her meeting with

Juana with a black eye. Juana, who at that time was driving for a councilman in Montevideo, showed up at her lover's house the next morning. The husband answered the door. He didn't even have time to say, 'good morning.' The big woman punched him in the mouth and then kicked him in the balls. The guy doubled over, and Juana hit him again. He fell backward. Do you know what Juana did then?"

"No idea."

"She unbuckled her belt, yanked it off quickly, and freed it from her pants. Then she sat on the guy's chest and started strangling him," said Rabbit with special emphasis on the last word. "Zulema tried to separate them but didn't have the strength to handle her lover. The driver kept tightening and tightening the belt, twisting the ends like a tourniquet to apply more pressure."

"So much drama, Rabbit! You talk as if you were there."

"Dude, it's all documented down to the smallest detail in the police report! Anyway, let me continue. The guy was a featherweight, a weakling with a ninety-five-kilo, one-meter-eighty tall woman choking him like a chicken."

"I'm not surprised, with those arms of hers," Adrián

commented.

"In the end, Zulema was rescued by neighbors who came running when they heard her hysterical screams. It took four of them to pull Juana off the guy. According to witnesses, Cardozo was already turning purple," Rabbit paused to catch his breath. "You should see the marks that were left on the poor guy's neck! I saw the photos attached to the file before you accuse me of exaggerating again."

"So, what happened then?" Adrián, now with a towel wrapped around his waist and the phone held between his cheek and shoulder, poured himself three fingers of black label.

"Cardozo pressed charges, and Juana was booked at headquarters for physical assault with intent to kill."

"Great work, Rabbit, you're a genius! I owe you one, man," Adrián said as he almost took the first sip of his Scotch.

"One? You owe me like a thousand, but I'll settle for a dinner at Morini or El Águila."

"At Morini or El Águila! Since when does a lowlife like you have such a refined palate?"

"Since I have a friend who earns in dollars. Come on, Fontana, stop being a cheapskate. How about we have dinner tonight?" Rabbit proposed with childlike enthusiasm.

"Tonight, I can't. I have a date at nine with a girl at Anticuario."

"Anticuario? That place is super trendy! I get it, first things first, and you look like you haven't scored in a while. We'll do it tomorrow then. And hey, I'm buying. Don't want you to get a heart attack."

"Sure. Take care, you clown. And thanks for the favor."

The detective hung up and took a hearty sip of Scotch. Then he got dressed and went out to smoke a cigarette on the balcony.

He knew Lucrecia didn't have the physical strength to strangle anyone. But Juana? Had the one-armed woman had an aggressive argument with Carlota while her driver was present in the penthouse? Did things get physical, and Juana's strong arms did the job her boss ordered? Was the altercation over Lucrecia's obsession with the white wolf painting, or was there a more powerful reason for the art dealer to silence Carlota forever? The painting's value was considerable, but would she really kill over thirty thousand dollars or whatever it was? Lucrecia seemed financially healthy. It didn't quite add up. Moreover, according to the press, the marks on Carlota's neck indicated that the strangulation had been done with a fine object, something that had almost cut the skin.

The detective stubbed out his cigarette on the balcony ledge and went back inside, scratching his head, lost in thought. Something still didn't fit. Or maybe it did, he thought. Even though Juana had an instinctive tendency to go for her victims' throats, perhaps this time she had been more sophisticated and used a rope, a chain, or a wire.

Adrián stood in front of the bathroom mirror and poured a generous amount of Agua Brava into the hollow of his hand. He slapped it on his face and behind his neck. He quickly rubbed his fingertips on his face to spread the fragrance and let the aroma refresh his nostrils. This ritual lifted his spirits, rejuvenating him. Sofía always accused him of overusing colognes, but he couldn't conceive of using Agua Brava sparingly.

He smoothed his hair forward, first with his nails and then with the palm of his hand. He could do without a comb since he kept it very short. He left the bathroom and opened the closet. He put on a beige suede jacket. The smell of aged leather from

Morocco brought back memories of his last case before Sofía hired him. He had bought the jacket in Casablanca with the leftover expenses allocated for tracking a Richmond banker through the Maghreb. He recalled Mrs. Ferguson's inconsolable crying later when he had returned to Richmond. The photos from his inseparable Nikon had confirmed her suspicions. Under the pretext of business trips, her husband was having an affair with his secretary in North Africa. The memory came back to him as he entered the elevator. A friendly old lady smiled at him. The detective greeted her with a nod and pretended to pet the Chihuahua she was holding, which triggered a hysterical outburst from the tiny excuse for a dog that didn't stop barking until the elevator doors opened on the ground floor.

Adrián stepped out onto the street and looked at his wristwatch. It was 8:30 PM, and he had half an hour to adhere to proper social etiquette. A gentleman should always arrive first.

The Anticuario bar was an old two-story house, restored to look like it did in the past. Soon after its opening, it had become the trendiest spot in Montevideo's nightlife. The name matched the nostalgic memorabilia displayed on its whitewashed brick walls and oak beams supporting the ceiling. Photos of Carlos Gardel, Julio Sosa, La Negra Rosa Luna, and Einstein's visit to Uruguay mingled in a nostalgic salad of luminaries who had set foot on national territory. There were also relics or musical instruments from other times, such as an old phonograph in a corner or a marble mortar on the bar for leaving tips for the grill master. Old copper buckets and all sorts of knick-knacks, probably acquired at the Tristán Narvaja market or in the city's auction houses, evoked the old Montevideo, summarizing what European immigrants had forged or brought to the shores of the Rio de la Plata. Unlike other Latin American countries where the Maya or Inca cultures still survived, the place didn't display Charrúa crafts. It made sense. The first president of the fledgling republic had taken care of exterminating them in the famous massacre of Salsipuedes during the first half of the nineteenth century, after the naive indigenous people had helped him and many others in the wars of independence.

Adrián Fontana arrived ten minutes before the meeting and chose a spot by the window. He ordered a black label while waiting for Graciela. The place was full of young couples displaying body language that hinted their parents had indulged their every whim. Lost in his thoughts, sitting with his legs to the side of the table, the detective smoked a Nevada, leaning forward, eyes on the old pinewood floor when he heard a "Hello!" voice. As he looked up, he lingered for a few seconds on the two sculptural legs, adorned with a tiny scrap of a miniskirt, planted in front of his table. Then he continued upward until he found her face.

"Hello, Graciela," Adrián said. He stood up and kissed her on the cheek. She smelled of good perfume, probably French, and was made up to highlight her sensual dark-skinned features, with subtle shadows on her eyelids, rouge on her cheeks, and vermilion on her lips.

"Cabotine?"

"Yes. How do you know?" she said. "I see you're quite the perfume expert."

"No, it's just that it was my ex's favorite. Sometimes I use it too."

"Oh, it must be your feminine sensitivity coming out," she said, teasing him.

"I wouldn't bet much on my feminine sensitivity, my dear," he laughed mockingly.

As they joked, he looked around again at the other tables and then back at her, who didn't stand out at all from the average age of the rest of the crowd. He felt like a fish out of water. There he was, at thirty-eight, trying to act cool with a girl who couldn't be more than twenty-five, he thought. The spark of a generation gap didn't deter his libido, still intact to face and dissolve any insinuation of puritan ethics that crossed his mind.

"What are you having?" he asked.

She opted for the black label and suggested ordering a juicy flank steak sliced into thin strips, which seemed to be the house specialty. The lively clientele made the conversations add decibels to a space too small for so many mouths talking simultaneously. "So typical of us Uruguayans," Adrián thought. He remembered the time he had traveled to Montevideo with an American friend. The northerner looked bewildered, trying to answer the avalanche of questions simultaneously from "Rabbit" Vergara, his mother, and his two sisters. He had also become unaccustomed to it, with so many years up north. Yet, he liked it. It was exorcising to immerse himself again in the clamor of his roots. The noise made him almost have to brush Graciela's cheek to speak or listen to her.

"Why are you getting so close?" she said, enjoying teasing him. "Did you forget your hearing aid at the hotel, old man?" she added, letting out a short, sharp giggle.

Adrián raised his eyebrows, resigning himself to the sarcasm. He smiled. He stared at her for a few seconds with his elbow on the table, holding his face in the palm of his hand. Then he asked:

"Do you know "Cheeks" Stern?"

"Who?" she reacted, surprised by the shift, after maintaining eye contact, studying his desire. She paused and asked, "The mobster? The one who breeds racehorses and has a Carnaval group?"

"The same."

"I saw him once here in the neighborhood during the "Llamadas" of the Carnival parade. He was leading the troupe Morenada, waving his hat to the crowd. He's a big fat guy."

"So, you live around here?"

"Yes, five blocks from here. That's why I suggested meeting at Anticuario. I walked over," she said. "If you want, later I can invite you to my apartment for a glass of Veuve Clicquot cognac, vintage 1966, a gift from a friend."

"Wow, you have expensive friends! That French pronunciation turned my hormones upside down. Let's see . . . say it again," he said, looking amused.

"Veu . . . ve Clic . . . quot," Graciela repeated slowly, forming a red rose with her lips. The girl knew how to play, Adrián thought.

"What do you do in the United States?"

"I break the hearts of wealthy married couples who want a picture of what they've long suspected of each other."

"You're a private detective?" Graciela exclaimed. "Wow, that's amazing! I've never dated a detective. What are you doing in Montevideo?"

"Pleasure, I told you," He whispered, keeping his eyes fixed on hers. Then he asked, "Do you know where "Cheeks" Stern lives?"

"No idea, but why are you so interested in that guy, Adrián? Are you also crime inclined?"

"No, but I'm something that ends in . . . ed."

Graciela laughed and looked at him questioningly.

"Sex-obsessed," he clarified, whispering in her ear. She let out a laugh. The waiter brought a platter of flank steak, seared on the outside and perfectly pink inside, sliced with scientific symmetry and accompanied by chimichurri and freshly baked bread, sliced into pieces.

"Enjoy," he said as he left, with a professional tone that matched his impeccable white uniform, black bowtie at the neck, and slicked-back hair held tightly with pomade.

"So many delicacies! I don't know where to start. The steak or the brunette?"

"Start with the steak. Save the brunette for dessert," Graciela suggested.

"Good idea," he said, attacking the first piece of meat with his fork and dipping it in the chimichurri.

"Should we get another whiskey or switch to red wine?" she asked.

"I'll stick with Mr. Walker, and you?"

"The same," said Graciela, who seemed to have more alcohol culture than Richard Burton. Between cigarettes and countless rounds of Scotch, sharing stories from the north and the south, midnight arrived. Graciela again suggested having dessert at her apartment, and they headed there, leaning on each other, happy, singing drunkenly. When they reached the corner of Tacuarembó and Isla de Flores, they heard a screeching behind them. Two large shadows got out of a car with no lights. At the same time, from the Isla de Flores side, Adrián noticed the sound of heels running. He saw the ambush coming.

"Run, girl!" he managed to say. She widened her eyes, and he felt the girl's body tremble. There were four of them, and they weren't there for a social call. He threw a left hook at the face of the first one who reached him, landing solidly between the nose and mouth. The big guy let out a nearly childish cry that didn't match his body. Adrián prepared to finish with a right hook but didn't have time. Another attacker punched him in the stomach, doubling him over. He fell to the sidewalk and took a kick to the head. He was dazed, almost unconscious. The thugs dragged him into the car. One of them blindfolded him, and another tied his hands with plastic zip ties like electricians use to bundle cables. He heard Graciela's terrified voice struggling with the other two. Then, he heard a slap sound. She went silent. They shoved her into the car. Graciela whimpered like a scared little mouse. The car's engine roared twice. The tires screeched on the cobblestones, and the car sped off, shifting from first to second and third gear in less than fifty meters. A small opening in the window let in the salt-laden wind. The detective deduced they were heading downhill towards the coast. He heard the waves crashing against the seawall when they made a sharp left turn onto the promenade, heading east. Graciela's body pulsed beside him.

"Relax, doll," one of them said. "This isn't about you. You won't get hurt."

The girl's lips kept trembling.

"Stop shaking, you bitch!" another voice said. Adrián heard a sound like a second slap. "We're only interested in this playboy you're with," he said, almost whispering in the detective's ear.

Adrián smelled the bad breath and sweaty body odor of the beast. He decided to deliver a solid head-butt to the side. He heard the crunch of teeth followed by a suppressed groan.

"Son of a bitch!" was the last thing he heard before losing consciousness to the barrage of punches that landed on the other side of the blindfold covering his face.

# XIX

THE FIRST THING HE smelled before opening his eyes was the stench of manure. Adrián Fontana was seated in the central aisle of a barn with a row of stables on either side, where the heads of a few horses peeked out. The cooing of pigeons came from the thatched roof's beams. His hands were tied to the back of a chair. He deduced he was in one of Alberto Stern's strongholds by the array of equines.

"If I'd been told I was invited to Cheeks's house, I would have dressed for the occasion," he said with difficulty. His lips felt numb as if he had just left the dentist, from the punches he had received in the car. In front of him was a bear of a man with a paleolithic head, eyes hidden between swollen eyelids, and extremely hairy eyebrows that almost joined in a straight line on his tiny forehead. The troglodyte, Adrián thought, was how he always imagined the transition from ape to the first hominid.

"Cut the jokes, kid!" said the subhuman and slapped him, rattling his molars.

"That's enough, King Kong, leave him to me," said someone behind the chair, patting the detective's back.

"King Kong? You certainly were named right! It suits your face," said Adrián.

The gorilla smacked him again, making him wobble in the chair.

"My mother hit harder, you moron!" Adrián retorted, his face flushed, letting out a furious laugh.

"King Kong! Stop it, damn it!" said the voice that hadn't yet come into view.

"But . . . boss," protested the ape-man, "leave him to me. I'll make this assface sing Ave Maria."

"Go . . . give some sugar cubes to Black Eight while I have a civilized conversation with the gentleman," ordered Cheeks, pointing towards one of the stables where the majestic head of a black stallion peeked out.

"Yeah, go ahead, monkey, animals understand each other," said Adrián, as King Kong walked towards the stable, grinding his teeth.

Then, "Cheeks" Stern placed the chair he was holding on the floor and sat in front of the detective. He was a bit more wrinkled but still had the physical traits Adrián remembered. Obese, pear-shaped, and enormously tall, just like his father. The flesh of his inflated cheeks was beginning to yield to gravity but still stood firm and healthy on his chubby face.

"Okay, brother . . . tell me what you were doing at my villa in Punta del Este," said "Cheeks" Stern, giving a nearly paternal smile as he patted the detective's knee. "You looked very photogenic on the cameras I have hidden among the neighbor's pines. What were you looking for?"

"And did the cameras also tell you my name and where to find me, or did your goddaughter's father, Commissioner Bermúdez, give you the tip?" Adrián replied.

"No, that's not the way to go, brother. The questions are only asked by the host. What were you doing peeking through the window? Because . . . you didn't break in. There was no broken glass or forced locks."

"I wanted to see how the rich decorate their summer villas. That's all, 'brother.'"

"Keep being funny, and I'll call King Kong, who surely won't caress your snout like he did Black Eight," said Stern. "I know you're investigating Carlota Ferraro's death, and you have my full sympathy and support for going after the scumbag who took her life, but you don't think I had anything to do with it, do you?"

"Well, you don't exactly have a reputation for being Mahatma Gandhi. Didn't you go too far with Carlota?" Adrián said, raising an eyebrow and smirking. He regretted it instantly as Cheeks's hand sprung up like a spring, gripping three-quarters of his neck.

"Look, you piece of shit, I adored that girl. Understand? She was the only one who moved me. So instead of wasting time snooping around my residence, you better sharpen your aim to find the culprit. Capisce?" he said, showing his nicotine-stained teeth.

"Wow! What a lovely brother!" Adrián muttered after Cheeks withdrew his hand, which had been cutting off his air. He coughed and swallowed the accumulated saliva.

"What were you looking for?" insisted the mafioso.

"I was looking for what I found. The painting of the white wolf, 'dear brother.' What the hell is Carlota's painting doing in your house? Sorry, but you don't exactly reflect sensitivity for art."

Cheeks stood up and began to pace in front of the detective. His eyes on the floor as if walking through memories. Then, fiercely, he locked eyes with Adrián again.

"The poor girl needed money, you idiot! She had burned through her entire fortune," he paused and softened his gaze. "She offered me the painting for $30,000. I lent her the money but didn't accept the painting. One weekend, we met at the villa, and she brought the painting. 'Take it,' she said, 'hang it here in the bedroom. We'll look at it when we make love. Besides, it'll be safer here. When I pay you back, you'll return it to me. I want to leave it to my sister who lives in the United States so at least she has a crumb of the family heritage.' Even though they hadn't spoken for years, she always told me that her sister was one of the few people she respected. 'Sofía is the only one who hasn't been corrupted by the Ferraro family's twists. The rest of us are all shit,' she said. Satisfied your curiosity, detective?"

"Are you going to fulfill the love of your life's wish and return the painting to her sister?" Adrián asked with his best cynical face.

"Do I look like an idiot? Did I get the $30,000 back? No! Then the painting stays with papa."

"I thought, since you rejected it at first, you might be interested in doing something for others."

"Screw others, detective!" the pear-shaped man exclaimed furiously. "Look . . . as a very special favor, I'm going to let you go with that girl you were playing hero with. My intuition tells me you're the best chance Carlota has for us to find who sent her to the grave. The cops are useless, and I'm not very aware of who she hung out with when she wasn't with me. She was very independent. Now then," he said, raising his index finger and voice, "a favor is paid with another favor. As soon as you discover who the bastard is, you tell me first. No police. Got it? And don't disappoint me, detective. I'm in a good mood today. You don't want to meet me when my blood's up. Go on . . ." he lowered his tone while untying his hands. "No hard feelings. Nothing happened here."

"Nothing happened here?" Adrián smiled while rubbing his wrists. "Can I twist King Kong's balls a bit before leaving, to go 'without hard feelings'?"

"Go on, leave. Don't try to be tough, you got off easy this time," said Cheeks, patting him on the shoulder.

For precaution, to protect the boss, King Kong approached, brandishing a .38 caliber. Adrián took a few steps to the threshold of the stable door. He squinted, momentarily blinded by the rays of the rising sun. He opened his eyes again, turned to Cheeks, and asked, "Don't you have a candy to throw to the cute little monkey who beat me up?"

King Kong prepared to charge like a bull, but the boss's look was enough to keep him rooted to the spot.

"Walk, kiddo, don't push your luck. Today, Don Stern is in a good mood," said the giant, winking. "If it were up to me, you'd be leaving feet first."

A smoked-glass Opel 2.0 approached the stable slowly. The driver, blonde, with a shaved head and a Slavic peasant face, got out of the vehicle and opened the back door. Graciela's face emerged from the car with the same terrified expression she had when she got in the night before. She ran to Adrián and clung to his chest as if starring in the melodramatic end of a 1930s movie. She was still trembling.

# XX

THE SKY, ORPHANED OF stars, slowly diluted as if an invisible brush were watering down the black watercolor of the firmament to the maximum. Timid, cautious, like a blonde child playing hide-and-seek, the sun was already starting to peek its head out of the sea, next to the Isle of Flowers. Fresh ochre lava spilled over its shoulders and began to spread across the horizon. Adrián checked his wristwatch. It was half past six. A vigorous southern wind pushed against the couple's backs as they ascended from the promenade to the hills of Palermo. Graciela rubbed her arms. The detective took off his suede jacket and offered it to the young woman. She smiled gratefully. Adrián took out a cigarette. He shielded the lighter's flame with his hand to protect it from the wind. He held the filter between his lips and embraced the young woman. She snuggled, fragile, against the detective's chest.

"At least they left us close by," said the brunette, as they were almost at the building where she lived.

"Yeah, a real treat, those Cheeks's gorillas. It's nice to be kidnapped like this," commented the detective after exhaling smoke. "I'll drop you off at your apartment and head to the hotel." When they arrived at the entrance, the doorman hadn't arrived yet. Graciela reached into her purse and found the key. She returned the jacket and turned to open the door.

"Aren't you coming up?" she asked with a suggestive look, pouting her lips playfully. "I still owe you dessert."

"Another day, kid. Go rest," he said, stroking her cheek. "Recover from the scare. We'll get in touch later."

Graciela stretched out and wrapped her arms around his neck, sheltering her head under the detective's chin for a moment. Then, she kissed the corner of his lips. Adrián resisted. He could still feel the punches from the early morning in his mouth. She insisted he come up so she could tend to his wounds. He refused again, promising to stop by a pharmacy. He waited for her to enter the elevator, put his jacket back on, and walked away uphill. As he headed to the hotel, a paradox kept ringing in his mind. Carlota wanted to give the painting of the white wolf to her sister instead of her son. That's not what parents usually do. Especially when the family's finances are in shambles. Don't they protect their offspring first? He understood that the Ferraro's eldest daughter might feel guilty towards her sister. She had always monopolized her parents' attention for her whims, but was this remorse strong enough to prioritize Sofía over Javier? Carlota appeared more enigmatic, with more shades of gray. Until now, he had always seen her in black and white. The executive Carlota, Donato Ferraro's right hand, the one who ruled her father's empire with an iron fist. He slept stiff as a corpse until two in the afternoon. The noise of an ambulance woke him up. He decided to wake up sitting on the shower floor, with the water pressure at its maximum. Relieving the bruises on his body. He tried to organize what had come out of Stern's mouth. Cheeks sounded believable, sincere. He knew Stern wasn't a little angel and might be wrong, but his reading of the mobster's body language led him to think he was telling the truth. He called Rabbit and they agreed to meet at El Yoruga at three-thirty in the afternoon. On his way down, he approached the counter to leave the key at reception. Another young woman replacing Graciela informed him that someone had left a note for him. He took it out of the envelope and read: "Hello, handsome, I need to see you urgently. I'll wait for you at eight-thirty in my apartment. There are developments in the case that will interest you. Hugs, Lucrecia." As he read, he felt the inquisitive gaze of the hotel manager at the periphery of his eyes, analyzing his face from the corner of the counter. He put the note in his pocket and preempted the question. "Nothing serious, Manuel. I popped a pimple above my lip, and it got infected," he said, accompanied by a smile. Manuel nodded but said nothing. He knew his guest didn't like nosy people. He also knew from previous trips about his tendency to get into fights, his drunken brawls when visiting Montevideo. Adrián patted his shoulder as he passed by. "Relax, old man. I appreciate the worried look, but it's nothing a good medication can't cure. And here I go, heading to El Yoruga, to disinfect myself with a

Johnny Walker." When he went out to the sidewalk, Manuel was still nodding.

Adrián sat where he always did. By the window. At that hour, the bar was almost empty. He ordered a long cappuccino and a ham and cheese croissant. He had skipped lunch and needed to put something in his stomach. While waiting for Rabbit, he lit a Nevada. He took out Lucrecia's note, smoothed it out, and read it again. What did the one-armed woman want to tell him? He put it away again. The waiter arrived with his order. He bit into the croissant enthusiastically and made a face of anger as he chewed. His jaw still remembered King Kong. He cursed the monkey man and fantasized about the possibility of facing him again on equal terms. Rabbit's arrival interrupted his revenge fantasies.

"What are you having, Vergara?"

"The usual," said Rabbit while hanging his jacket on the back of the chair.

"Waiter, two whiskeys and a Coke with ice."

"And who is the Coke for?" reacted Rabbit, squinting his eyes.

"For you. The whiskey to bring the blood back to your body after what I'm going to tell you, and the Coke to fix your stomach when you get the runs."

He described in detail his meeting with "Cheeks" Stern. Rabbit Vergara turned as white as a wax doll.

"And did he ask about me?" inquired Vergara, wide-eyed.

"Calm down, man. I don't think he connects you with me or knows we're friends."

"And when he finds out? Because sooner or later he will!"

"Again, with this, man? We already talked about it. You tell him we were schoolmates, and that's it."

"Stop being so naive to think Cheeks is an idiot."

"He won't do anything to you, Vergara. The fat guy is a bad guy but has a well-developed sense of smell. He knows how to distinguish between wild beasts and harmless farm pets. You belong to the second group, fool," he concluded with a mocking grin.

"Go to hell, Fontana. You always take everything as a joke."

They continued talking. Occasionally, the detective looked at a mirror hanging on a column. A gray-haired man with a sunken face had entered a few minutes earlier. Positioned at a table near the entrance, he was reading a newspaper. Adrián had a good nose for distinguishing between regular customers and those who sat at a table like he had done so many times at Richmond to track an unfaithful spouse.

"And now, what's your next move?" said Rabbit after emptying his glass.

"I don't know yet. Maybe visit Carlota's son again or go annoy Commissioner Bermúdez. Anything to stir things up. In troubled waters, fishermen profit, Vergara."

"Well, it's up to you and your troubles, but be careful. Remember, in this country, you don't mess with the cops or the military."

Adrián agreed with Rabbit. Otherwise, he wouldn't have kept him so informed. He needed a witness to his steps. He knew his life wasn't guaranteed.

"Pay and let's go, Vergara. It's your turn today."

Rabbit left the money under a dish with the bill. They both headed for the exit. When Adrián passed by the table of the sunken-faced man, he peeked over the newspaper and took a photo with his cell phone.

"Hey, at least change the page from time to time so it's not so obvious you're following me. Give my regards to Commissioner Bermúdez," he said while flicking his lit cigarette onto the table. The other man just stared at him without saying anything. Rabbit Vergara stood frozen. When they walked out the door, he was still more confused than Adam on Mother's Day. The detective said goodbye to his friend and returned to the hotel. He thought his body would appreciate two or three more hours of rest before meeting with Lucrecia. At eight-fifteen, he was already extinguishing his cigarette in the sand-filled ashtray beside the elevator of the Palacio Salvo. He closed the noisy gate and pressed the button for the 17th floor. When he got off the metal cage, he noticed that Lucrecia's door was ajar. He drummed two short knocks with his knuckles to announce himself.

"Lucrecia?" he said, poking his head inside. No response. He decided to enter. He called her name again, raising his voice a bit more. Total silence. He crossed the small entrance hall and stopped abruptly upon reaching the living room, as if paralyzed by an electric shock. Lucrecia lay with her head thrown back over the back of the sofa, as if she wanted to look at him upside down. She was undoubtedly dead. Her eyeballs nearly bulged out of their sockets, frozen in a horrible expression. Her single arm hung down the side of the sofa, with her hand curled like a spider. He noticed the bottle of vodka toppled over on the shattered glass of the coffee table. Perhaps due to the kicks she had given while struggling for her life. The television was tuned to a Spanish cable channel broadcasting the Eurovision Song Contest. A very thin, purple line circled her strangled, tightly compressed neck. There was no doubt. She had been strangled. Her incisors were sunk into her tongue, which barely protruded from her mouth in what must have been a final desperate attempt to bite the life escaping her. He stared at her for a moment, trying to decipher the secret of her stiff irises, which looked without seeing, in a terrified clownish grimace. Despite having her on his list of suspects until that moment, he couldn't avoid feeling some remorse. He hadn't even thanked her for saving his life. He closely observed her clenched fingers. They seemed to have strips of bloody flesh caught under their nails. He glimpsed a clue for forensic analysis: perhaps they belonged to the face of the executioner. He straightened up and walked to the desk where the phone was. He dialed 911 and reported the discovery. A box full of opened mail caught his attention. "Junk mail," he murmured after a few seconds, realizing it was nothing relevant. That's how they called the advertising flyers that overflowed mailboxes in the

United States. He took a handkerchief from his back pocket to avoid leaving fingerprints and tried to open the desk drawer. It was locked but there was no key in sight. Perhaps he could rule out robbery as a motive for the crime. Anyway, this was his best chance to see what the one-armed woman kept locked up before the police arrived. He looked around, searching for something to open it with. The firewood poker next to the stove. That would be enough to pry open the lock. He held the iron bar with the handkerchief. The oak yielded without difficulty. Inside the drawer were some recently dated invoices. Beneath them, an envelope with a Spanish postmark. The letter was still inside. The sender had an address in Barcelona. Lucio López - Appraisal of art and antiques. Adrián unfolded the note and read: "Dear Mrs. Lucrecia, According to our previous conversations, I am in a position to confirm almost certainly, after observing the photograph you attached, that the painting of the white wolf is by Alfred Kowalski, a 19th-century Polish painter (1849–1915), famous for his wolf scenes. The painting disappeared from a German collector's mansion after the Allied victory in 1945. If its authenticity can be confirmed, the work could be worth over two hundred fifty thousand euros. Let us know as soon as you have the painting, and we will travel to Montevideo with our team of experts to conduct the necessary technical investigations. Yours sincerely, Lucio López."

Adrián put the letter back in the envelope and slipped it into the inside pocket of his jacket. Then he faced Lucrecia, as if she were still alive.

"Is that it, one-armed? Were you hell-bent on getting the white wolf, and Juana took care of killing Carlota? Or did you tell the secret to a third party who killed her when he couldn't get the painting's whereabouts from her? And now you paid for your indiscretion with your life?"

Lucrecia didn't seem loose tongued. She was street-smart and cautious. "Too far-fetched. It doesn't fit," he concluded. Then he chewed on another conjecture. Cheeks Stern! Maybe he knew the painting was worth a fortune. Carlota demanded the painting, and he killed her. Then somehow Lucrecia found out he had the painting at his chalet in Punta del Este and tried to blackmail him. Did Cheeks decide to silence her too?

"Is that what you wanted to talk to me about, Lucrecia? To help you recover the painting."

But no, that didn't fit either. If Stern was the killer, why did he let him go in the stable? Unless Bermúdez had told his daughter's godfather that 'the nosy detective was an American citizen.' The commissioner would have warned Cheeks that he didn't want the Yankees breathing down the neck of the Police Headquarters. This didn't sound viable either. He couldn't see Cheeks being influenced by a corrupt cop when it came to leaving no loose ends. As he continued immersed in hypotheses, Lucrecia's tragicomic expression seemed to mock his speculations. She, who perhaps had the answer and had taken it to the grave. Adrián walked a few steps to the bar, next to the window, and poured himself a double Johnny Walker. He sat facing the art dealer's corpse and raised his glass.

"Cheers, one-armed. For now, I give you the benefit of the doubt. For better or worse, you had cojones, as they say in your land. See you on the other side, to settle accounts or have a drink."

# XXI

SHE PAUSED TO BLOW her nose. She was a strong woman, but the murder of Lucrecia had disarmed her. Sitting across from Adrián in the La Pasiva brewery, beneath the colonnade of the Palacio Salvo, Juana bit her lower lip to keep tears from flooding her brown eyes. It had been a long time since she had run out of the tears a body can produce. Her son was listed among the disappeared during the military dictatorship. Dried out in life for a long time, numbed of emotions, now her eyes were wet again. The detective placed a hand on the shoulder of the corpulent woman.

"Lucrecia is with God now, woman," he said, not out of religious conviction but because he couldn't think of anything else. The driver raised her head, her expression hard.

"Don't come to me with God, Adrián! That man is always on vacation while Satan is feasting down here in this miserable world. Murderers! To torment a disabled person like that."

"Do you have any idea who it might have been?" Adrián asked, wiping the beer foam from his mustache.

"No idea. It could be so many . . . Lucrecia had a strong character and surely made many enemies."

"Do you think Bonilla could be behind the crime? I remember Lucrecia was helping you and the mothers of the disappeared."

"Lucrecia wasn't as involved as we were. She just offered logistical support. She wasn't an activist or anything like that."

"But . . . had she discovered something important related to Carlota's murder? She left me a note at the hotel."

"I don't know. She didn't tell me everything. Sometimes she opened up, but generally, she was reserved by nature. She must have sensed something that put her on alert."

"But . . . I thought you two also had a romantic relationship."

"No, man," Juana said, clicking her tongue and shaking her head. For a moment, the anguish disappeared from her face, and she smiled. "You men are so funny. When you see two lesbians together, the first thing you assume is that they sleep in the same bed. I wasn't her type, and she wasn't mine. It's like if I thought you slept with your friend the buck-toothed one, just because you're both in the same line of work."

Adrián smiled and nodded, conceding to the irrefutable logic.

"You're right, pure idiosyncratic deformation. Excuse my nonsense."

"Lucrecia was an alpha. She liked to dominate, just like me. We would have skinned each other alive if we lived together," Juana commented, raising her eyebrows as she rummaged through her bag. She took out a box of La Paz Suave and tapped it twice on her wrist to release a cigar. She lit it, closed her eyes, and inhaled deeply. She exhaled a long puff and stayed thoughtful, looking at the floor. After a few seconds, she started running her hand against the grain of her short hair. She lifted her eyes, convinced, and bristled.

"It must be Bonilla! When I told Lucrecia about my son's disappearance, she thought she could help me and the other mothers. We knew from some survivors that Bonilla liked to film his torture sessions. Lucrecia knew that Carlota had been his lover. Lucrecia thought she might get a secret from Carlota that would lead us to find the bodies of our boys. I'm sure that son of a bitch killed Carlota first and then Lucrecia to tie up loose ends. We must crush that cockroach once and for all. To hell with the law," Juana said, pounding her bear paw on the table.

"Calm down, woman. His time will come. Would you be capable of killing?"

"For justice? Without a hair trembling!" Juana said, gritting her teeth.

"There's something curious about both crimes," Adrián said, scratching his chin.

The driver's eyes lit up. "What?" she demanded, motivated, leaning forward to rest her elbows on the table.

"The same method to kill. The killer has a weakness for necks," Adrián said, studying the driver's pupils. For a moment, he thought he had touched a nerve, but Juana responded with a look of sufficiency.

"What's so strange about that? If Bonilla hired a killer, surely the bastard operates the same way every time."

"You're right, woman," Adrián said, putting on his best clueless face. "If I keep this up, they'll revoke my detective license for mental slowness," he added, hitting his forehead. He had learned a long time ago that sometimes the truth comes out by playing the fool. The other lowers their guard and falls into the trap. But this wasn't the case with Juana. She remained planted in front of him as if nothing.

"Who left me the note at the hotel, you or Lucrecia?"

"She wrote it in the car and asked me to go down and leave it at the reception."

"And what did you do after that?"

"I took her home. We had lunch together. At two in the afternoon, she went to take a nap. She told me to take the rest of the day off."

"I found her dead at eight-thirty, so she was killed approximately between the nap and eight at night. Where were you during those hours?"

Juana raised her chin and stared like a laser into the detective's eyes. Without trying for a moment to look away. She didn't even blink.

"I took the car to be washed at the station on Maldonado and Ejido and then went home," she paused, leaned back in the chair, and narrowed her eyes. "Why so many questions? Do you suspect me?"

"No, Juana, it's not that. I'm just asking. Pure professional deformation. Besides, you'd better be prepared for these questions. They'll be the same ones the police will ask you."

A loud flapping of pigeons, competing for the crumbs thrown by some retirees sitting in Plaza Independencia, diverted the driver's eyes. She seemed to relax her body and fell silent for a few minutes, her face afflicted, returning to her sorrow. Still looking at the plaza, she reflected aloud: "Lucrecia had a very good sense for people. She didn't like the maid. She didn't trust her. She said she was a woman of bad character."

"Who, Consuelo?" Adrián reacted, widening his eyes. "But she's a saint! A wretched woman who spent her life enduring humiliations from the Ferraro clan."

"Well, Lucrecia didn't like her. Especially after she caught her spying while she was talking to Carlota about a painting, she wanted to buy from her. A few days ago, we had seen her sitting on the boardwalk hugging a fisherman, and she made me stop the car."

"A fisherman?"

"Yes, a much older man than her. He was holding the fishing rod in one hand and hugging her by the waist. Lucrecia lowered the window a few centimeters to study them better." Juana paused and lit another cigarette.

"And then?" Adrián said, leaning on the table, with his chin resting between his hands.

"'Look at the sly one,' she commented under her breath and ordered me to drive away."

The detective's mind was now working on two simultaneous tracks. He was making conjectures while concentrating on every word, every facial expression of Juana. He remembered asking Consuelo if she had a boyfriend or had gotten married. He justified that maybe she was embarrassed to confess a relationship with an older man. Or perhaps she was jealous of her privacy.

Juana changed the subject and asked if he had read the note left at the hotel. Adrián explained that Lucrecia only wanted to see him. The driver studied his eyes. The detective took a long sip from the beer jug. He felt for the pack of Nevada cigarettes in the inner pocket of his jacket. He struck the lighter wheel three times against the stone, which sparked without lighting. Juana stretched her arm across the table and offered the flame of hers. Adrián lit the tobacco and took a long drag. He turned in the chair and crossed one leg. He looked towards the imposing equestrian statue of Artigas in the middle of the plaza and exhaled the smoke through his nose. He remained silent for a few seconds. Then he turned back and asked casually:

"By the way, there's something I never asked you: Were you already working for Lucrecia when Carlota was killed?"

Juana narrowed her eyes. "I've been working for Lucrecia for over a year. What's this about?"

Adrián responded with another question: "When Lucrecia visited the deceased, did you go with her to the penthouse?"

"No, I stayed in the car. Why?"

"For nothing, woman. Just to know if you had observed anything that caught your attention in the apartment." The detective shook the beer jug to revive the foam and drank it in one gulp. He drummed on the table and stood to suggest ending the meeting.

"Thank you, Juana. Everything you've told me is very interesting. Now you should go rest," Adrián said, patting her shoulder as she also rose from the chair.

"What did this woman tell you?" interrupted the voice of Commissioner Bermúdez, who had approached silently like a cat. The chief had just raided the crime scene on the 17th floor of the Palacio Salvo with his men. Leaving the elevator, he had spotted the pair sitting outside under the building's monumental columns. He positioned himself between Juana and Adrián. "If it has to do with the crime, I must know."

"Oh, surprise, surprise. Commissioner Bermúdez!" Adrián said with a mocking grimace.

"What did she tell you, my friend?" Bermúdez insisted.

"How nice! Now we're friends? Well, see, nothing related to this case, but if it were, from this mouth: niente!" Adrián said, running his finger over his lips as if closing a zipper.

"I remind you that withholding information is a crime. Don't they teach that to detectives graduated in Gringolandia?"

"Indeed, and they also recommend having a good memory," Adrián replied.

"What do you mean?" the commissioner asked.

"A few days ago, you told me that the police do not share information with foreign detectives. Well, it also works the other way around, 'my friend,'" Adrián said, emphasizing the last word.

"I could arrest you for insubordination to authority."

Adrián smiled. Then he pulled out a photocopy of his passport from his jacket and held it up to the commissioner's eyes.

"You would be arresting a U.S. citizen, 'my esteemed commissioner.' I would be forced to resort to my embassy, and if we make too much noise, who knows what comes to light from the Montevideo backroom. And I take this opportunity to give you some advice. When you have me followed, at least instruct that skinny, malnourished, and foolish guy to be more discreet."

"I don't know what you're talking about, but as you wish, Fontana. Between firefighters, we don't step on each other's hoses," Bermúdez replied in a jocular tone. He started to turn towards 18 de Julio Avenue but stopped halfway and added with a mocking smile: "I see you insist on playing with fire. You're an unconventional firefighter. I'll pray that your ranch doesn't catch fire."

Adrián responded with the same type of smirk as the uniformed man. Then he turned to Juana, who was still looking at the commissioner with disgust.

"Come on, Juana, I'll give you a ride home. I'm parked around the corner."

She refused, but he insisted with his protective gesture. It was convenient for him that the driver kept thinking he wasn't the enemy. Besides, he had mixed feelings about the big woman. He still didn't rule out that she might know how much the white wolf painting was worth. And she might have betrayed the one-armed woman, now operating in partnership with a third party, or alone. All this didn't quite add up, but his thoughts were still influenced by Juana's background. She had tried to strangle the man who mistreated her lover, not with her hands but with a belt. Then, two murders carried out more or less in the same way. However, he was irritated to admit that at times he perceived something honorable, dignified, in the driver's body language. In the frank way she looked. This was in stark contradiction to the sleuth discipline instilled in him at the academy. A detective distrusts even his mother. However, Adrián deeply hoped that Juana was not involved.

# XXII

"I Can't Get No Satisfaction" made the speakers of Javier Ferraro's Opel tremble. The young man bobbed his head frenetically to the rhythm of the Rolling Stones as he drove east along the coastal road. His surfboard was strapped to the roof. His friends were waiting for him to ride the steep waves that formed at the curve of the boulevard, where the Punta Gorda neighborhood descends towards Playa de los Ingleses.

Adrián Fontana followed him closely, not getting too near. He had decided it was time to see Lieutenant Colonel Bonilla's face and was trying to coax or force Javier into revealing how to contact the former dictator. He suspected the military man had agreed to be the boy's godfather to please his mother. He remembered that during the times of the dictatorship, Carlota liked to be seen surrounded by the uniformed men. She must have seen the convenience of Javier being the godson of one of the members of the military junta that had the population by the balls.

The young man parked the vehicle in front of the dense shrubs that rose like a green wall from the sand, above the edge of the boulevard. He entered the thicket and used the density of the foliage to take off his pants and shirt and put on his wetsuit. He ran to join the group of surfers floating, waiting for the right wave. The detective got out of the car with a wire hanger in his hand. He stood in front of the Opel's window, dismantled the hanger, and stretched it out, leaving only the hook. He inserted the makeshift device between the rubber seal and the glass and began trying to hook the interior lock button. On the fourth attempt, he managed to lift it. That curve of the boulevard wasn't very frequented by pedestrians, allowing him to operate undisturbed. He estimated there would be an hour and a half of daylight left. The group would come out of the water before nightfall. He returned to his car and turned on the radio. He tuned to Océano FM and to kill time, he started listening to the show "Bad Thoughts." The host, Orlando Petinatti, seemed like an unpleasant guy, but Adrián was amused by the absurdities of the listeners who called the station. It was his way of re-immersing himself in the idiosyncrasies of his people, a tribe increasingly distant but still alluring.

As forecasted, when it started to get dark, the surfers came out of the water. They began to disperse toward their cars or into the neighborhood streets. Adrián got out of his car. He opened the rear door of the Opel and lay down on the back seat. He smiled, seeing that Javier had made his task easier. The mirrored windows of the vehicle didn't allow anyone to see inside. When the young man entered the car, the detective grabbed him by the hair, turning his head so he could see him. He pressed a switchblade against his cheek. Javier's eyes widened, and he had the urge to scream. Adrián discouraged him by pressing the knife harder into his flesh.

"Don't even think about opening that little mouth, okay? I'm getting old, and my hand shakes. Start the car and drive until I tell you," ordered the detective.

He pulled the switchblade back a few centimeters and let the young man's head return to its normal position.

Pale, with trembling lips, Javier stuttered: "What are you going to do to me? I haven't done anything . . ."

"Just a few questions. If you behave, you'll be screwing your girlfriend tonight. Otherwise, I'll cut your balls off and feed them to the crabs. Move it!" insisted the detective, reinforcing the command with a slap to the back of the neck.

They continued along the curve of the boulevard. After passing the last chalets and reaching Plaza Virgilio, Adrián ordered him to stop. The location was ideal. At that time of year, after the summer season, the place was deserted. He thought it was advantageous to have the empty field of the plaza to his left and to his right the rocks that cut off the occasional walk along the shore by a retired person walking their dog or a couple of lovers.

"Let's talk about that charming godfather of yours, Lieutenant Colonel Bonilla," said the detective. He extended his arms and rested them on the young man's shoulders.

"I don't know anything about Bonilla . . ."

Another slap to the back of the neck made him continue.

"He's just my godfather. I see him from time to time."

"Uh, let's see . . ." threatened Adrián, now inserting the tip of the switchblade into Javier's nostril. "If you keep messing with me, before I cut your balls off, I'll mess up that cute little nose that I'm sure the girls love. I know for a fact that you're his godson and that you have a close relationship with him. Close enough to ask him to have his men mess up my face."

"I only asked him to scare you. I swear, I didn't . . ." said Javier, almost crying, on the verge of a nervous breakdown.

"Calm down, kid," said Adrián, patting his head. "Tell daddy everything, and nothing will happen to you. Why does the lieutenant colonel keep helping you? After all, he was no longer with your mother when she was killed. What did Carlota know about him? Had she seen the torture video?"

"What video?"

"The torture video, kiddo. Your godfather filmed what he did to the political prisoners. Your mother knew too, and when the business went under, she needed money and started blackmailing him. Is that it?"

"You're crazy. He would have killed us!"

"Us?"

Javier cursed his use of the plural.

"I mean that . . ."

A loud slap on the cheek didn't let him finish.

"What do you know about the video?" said Adrián, pressing the knife's edge. In the rearview mirror, Javier saw his wolf-like eyes, ready to bite his neck.

"Bonilla will kill me if he knows I have the tape!" he sobbed, inconsolable.

The detective softened his tone.

"I'm only interested in catching your mother's killer. I won't involve you."

This last phrase, uttered with an almost paternal tone, seemed convincing. Javier made an effort to compose himself. He took a deep breath, straightened up a bit in his seat, looked out the windshield with eyes resigned to the horizon, and began the story:

"I found the video by accident. I had decided to hide cocaine in my mother's penthouse, in the air conditioning duct. When I opened the vent, I reached in to put the package deep inside and felt a lump. It was the tape.

I took it to my apartment and watched it. My mother had cut off the money she was giving me monthly. She said she was broke and that I had to find a job. The tape was my chance to keep receiving her help."

"You decided to blackmail her."

Javier lowered his head, seemingly ashamed, but the detective was certain that the son of the deceased woman didn't spend even half a second on guilt or remorse.

"She appeared in some scenes," Javier continued, losing his gaze beyond the windshield again. "She didn't participate. She smoked and drank whiskey, sitting on a couch, watching the tortures. She had given me money to pay the rent, but I lost it at the casino. I asked for more. We argued, both furious. She said she couldn't support me anymore. I insulted her, and she slapped me. My blood boiled. I told her that if she didn't give me money, I'd give the video to the press. Then she started screaming and threatening me. She'd ask her lover, the Jew Stern, to make me disappear. I warned her that I had already given instructions to a friend that if anything happened to me, he should send the tape to the communists. It was a lie. Nobody knows I have the video. My mother threw her whiskey glass at me and then the bottle. She was beside herself and kept throwing everything she had at hand."

"And what did you do?"

"I left. I figured that as long as she thought I had copies of the tape, she wouldn't retaliate. I let a few days pass to give her time to get the money. I knew she was having trouble with the business and had filed for bankruptcy."

"And you still blackmailed her," Adrián commented, winking and making a cynical smirk with his lips.

"What was I supposed to do? I was desperate. If I didn't pay the rent, they'd evict me from the apartment, and she wasn't Mother Teresa either. She had witnessed those tortures," Javier said, raising his voice.

"Okay, go on, and don't get worked up, or I'll give you another slap. What happened next? Did she give you the money?"

"No. That was the last time I saw her. A few days later, the phone rang. I thought it was her and ran to answer. It was the police. They had found her dead in her apartment."

"What a lovely family!" Adrián said, scratching his neck. "Good thing Sofía distanced herself from all this filth. Alright, start the car; let's go to your apartment."

"My house? Why?"

"I want to see the video."

"If Bonilla finds out I, have it, I'm a dead man."

"And since when do you have a certificate of manhood? Come on, start the car, idiot, before I change my mind and decide to split you in half like a pig. The whole world would benefit."

Javier started to open his mouth to offer more resistance, but the slap he received on his face convinced him that the smartest thing to do was to turn the key and start the engine.

# XXIII

A RUSTED TIN LAMP, shaped like a bell, hangs half a meter above the prisoner's head. A cone of warm light, invaded by cigarettes' smoke, envelops his silhouette. His hands are tied to the back of the chair. Around him, in the dim light, blurry faces can be seen, occasionally illuminated by cigarette embers.

Every so often, the prisoner cries. It's almost a child's cry. He glances sideways at the two men standing on either side of the chair, then at the one in front of him. He begs them not to hit him anymore. He shakes his head from side to side to rid himself of the sweat mixed with blood trickling down his face.

"Well, kid, it's your choice. Do you sing, or do we keep smashing the piñata?" says the one in front of him, pulling his hair back.

"I don't know anything. I swear on my mother. I already told you. I just joined the party when I entered college. I never got involved with the tupas," he insists, stammering with his split lips. He wants to say more, but he doesn't have time. A shadow standing behind the unfortunate soul places a transparent plastic bag over his head. It tightens around his neck. The wretch's eyes widen. He writhes desperately like a fish out of water. He emits a horrible, otherworldly, guttural sound. The bag collapses and shrinks around his nose and mouth. The suction is so strong that the more he gasps for air, the more the plastic clings to his face. The vicious cycle continues until his tormentors deem it enough and remove the hood. Gasping, he opens his mouth wide. His lungs expand and contract in rapid succession. He feels his chest explode. They leave him for a few minutes to collect the air stolen from him. They step back a few meters. One of them takes out a pack of cigarettes and offers it to the others. They decide to take a break and sit down to chat in the shadows. Someone with a high-pitched voice complains about a denied promotion and starts ranting against his boss. The others mock him.

Sitting in the living room, with Javier at the other end of the sofa, Adrián continues studying the video. He tries to make out the faces of the torturers, but they are shrouded in the strategic lighting focused on the prisoner.

The sinister tape keeps running. Now a door in the back opens. The detective's sharp eyes are reflected on the TV screen.

A burly man, with a firm step, a square head, and broad shoulders, approaches the prisoner from behind. He comes close enough to almost brush his cheek and whispers something in his ear. Now the light reveals his face. He doesn't seem to care. Lieutenant Colonel José Garvazzo, alias "El Niño," is beyond good and evil. He has made a pact with the devil and despises his colleagues who hide in the shadows. He couldn't care less about precautions. His fundamentalist crusade against the "Bolsheviks" justifies everything. He envisions a de facto regime that will last a thousand years and purge the communist infection from Latin America. The giant arm of "Operation Condor" reaches every corner of the Southern Cone. He oversees the Uruguayan branch: the sinister sect of planned disappearance and extermination that will ensure the homeland's soil is cleansed of any leftist filth.

Adrián pauses the video. He studies Garvazzo's features, his distinctive smile. He recognizes them. He has heard and seen enough of him in the years following the dictatorship. He knows that in the present, the civilian government has cornered him. Accusations from tortured survivors by the military are rampant. Adrián recalls that in 1995, after the resurgence of democracy, Garvazzo was convicted of extortion. Later, in 2002, while visiting Montevideo to see his mother, Adrián saw him again on television. The appeals court had modified the charge, sentencing him to ten months in prison.

So, there he was, once again starring on the screen, frozen by the pause button of the video recorder. Caught red-handed in his demonic task. Adrián presses the play button again.

Garvazzo walks around the prisoner and ends up standing in front of him, with his back to the camera. He offers him a glass of water. The tortured man closes his eyes as if thanking the gesture. Then the lieutenant colonel drops the glass. He quickly raises and extends his muscular arms to the sides of the victim's head. Suddenly, he closes them with a brutal and dry clap of his palms over the prisoner's ears. A pitiful scream escapes from the video player's speaker. Despite it being the second time, he has watched the recording, Carlota's son blinks at the scream. The detective, on the other hand, clenches his teeth and fist. He keeps his eyes fixed on the screen, witnessing the torture commonly known as "the phone." The door opens again. The silhouette of a couple contrasts. A man and a woman.

"Hello, Yamandú. Everything okay?" says Garvazzo. "Who is the broad?"

Bonilla's shadow moves toward the camera but keeps a sufficient distance to escape the cone of light.

"She's my girlfriend. Do you mind if she comes in? She wants to watch. She's curious to see how we do our patriotic duty," says Bonilla, releasing a hyena-like laugh.

"El Niño" Garvazzo shrugs, raises his eyebrows, and twists his thin mouth, almost lipless, to the side, indicating he couldn't care less.

"Go ahead, miss. Come in and take a seat. The show will continue in a few minutes," he comments, flashing his mold-made smile again.

Adrián approaches the TV, focused on the female shadow, with his index finger ready to press the pause button again.

Carlota moves across the room and sits a few meters from the victim. She is still shrouded in darkness, but Adrián recognizes her body language. Only one woman could walk like that. At that moment, something happens that reaffirms his conviction. The video recorder operator, undoubtedly an amateur judging by the shaky camera, stops focusing on the prisoner and turns toward Carlota. He does a close-up and bingo! There she is, captured in the foreground, the eldest daughter of the Ferraro family. Satisfying her morbid curiosity, sitting in front of what will undoubtedly be a future corpse, thrown from a plane into the muddy waters of the Río de la Plata. Delighting in the punishment of the much hated "bolches." Those she had often confronted in her executive days when her father sent her to face the union leaders at management meetings.

Bonilla approaches Garvazzo.

"Go ahead, José, take a break. I'll take over."

"But I just got here," protests Garvazzo, letting out a huff. "I'm fresh, hehe!"

"Go on, take a seat for a bit," insists Bonilla, eager to showcase his omnipotence to his new love conquest, in case she ever decides to betray him. He gestures to the other three, still smoking in the shadows.

"Come on, soldiers! Stop lazing around, damn it! Strip the comrade and tie him to the stretcher. Let's move, move, we don't have all night!"

The wretched man doesn't resist as they drag him like a sack of potatoes to the hellish cot. The energy, the survival instinct, has almost drained from his body. He is a lifeless lump, devoid of curiosity or panic about the next stage.

Bonilla approaches his girlfriend and starts kissing her with his plump mouth. A thin mustache contrasts with the thickness of his lips, accentuating his slimy demeanor. Then he approaches the naked body on the stretcher and gives it affectionate pats on the thighs.

"I know you're not asleep, fool, but if I'm wrong, you'll wake up now," he murmurs, letting out a sordid laugh. He grabs the electric terminals and touches them together to test the sparks. One of the soldiers splashes a ladle of water over the subjected man's body. Bonilla brings the terminals close to the scrotum. At that precise moment, Antonio Manzanares, the innocent agronomy student who had registered with the communist party almost out of naivety, out of curiosity, to please his girlfriend, out of youthful rebellion, feels firsthand, live and direct, what he had heard so many times only secondhand: the brutal procedure of the electric cattle prod.

He convulses like an epileptic, and his eyes roll back, filling the room with dreadful screams. No one can hear him beyond the walls of that chamber of hell. Garvazzo has ensured the room is soundproofed.

Carlota blinks once. Then she takes a cigarette from the case, lights it, and exhales the smoke slowly. The speakers Javier has placed next to the TV distort and crackle with the sharp cries of the wretch. Adrián violently presses the stop button.

"Enough. This is more than enough to illustrate the kind of scum your mother was. What rotten blood runs through your veins, kid!" says the detective, making a gesture as if to hit Javier but restrains himself. The young man covers himself with his hands. Adrián turns around and thinks of Sofía. What cruelty, what sadness for her to find out who her sister had been involved with. On the other hand, the military man deserves to be behind bars, and the video is the perfect passport to achieve it.

Will he tell Sofía? His first instinct says no. However, there is something he is sure of when he leaves Javier's apartment. Not even Satan himself will be able to prevent his next meeting with Bonilla. Adrián already anticipates the rage, the fear of the beast when he learns that he is in possession of the video that catches him red-handed, hands dirty before the whole Uruguayan society. Bonilla will foresee his children disgusted by the monster that fathered them. He will envision the disappointment in his grandchildren's eyes. The face of the demon behind the mask of a tender grandfather. Adrián salivates at the thought of the torturer tormented. The boomerang from the darkest time in Uruguayan history that now returns, at the dawn of the twenty-first century, to embed itself in Bonilla's forehead.

# XXIV

UNLIKE IN THE UNITED States, where golf courses are scattered across middle-class neighborhoods, in Uruguay, the sport was limited to the aristocracy. However, to survive modern times, the Golf Club of Punta Carretas decided to welcome both financially secure families and those who had lost much of their fortune. Its elegant Victorian-style tea room was the perfect excuse for social gatherings of double-barreled surnames. This old guard of blue blood came starched in body and soul to stir the ashes of their noble titles and continue to dream of a bygone era. Nevertheless, they still retained a treasure in their meager coffers: an immaculate intellect and a highly precise radar that allowed them to distinguish and look down on the "new rich;" those undesirable outsiders who parked their latest-model Mercedes Benz and BMWs right under their noses. Bonilla, who belonged to the fourth generation of a patrician family, had suggested that the club be the meeting place. Nothing could be more prudent than meeting the detective in his element, sheltered under the cypresses, eucalyptus, and casuarinas of the park's grove, far from microphones, hidden cameras, or witnesses. While he waited, he practiced from the tee box to kill time, accompanied only by his caddie. He didn't want to alarm the busybody who had dared to dig into his murky past.

As Adrián drove, he replayed his conversation from the previous night, when Bonilla had called him at the Hermitage. "Mr. Fontana, a little bird told me that you compile police-themed videos," the lieutenant colonel had said after introducing himself. "I am also an avid collector of fiction series and would be interested in purchasing a particular one from you. Could we meet to discuss it?"

"And doesn't your godson, that little bird, fear that you might pluck him or wring his neck for hiding the existence of such a valuable video?" Adrián had replied. "This particular video is not a product of fantasy, but a documentary made in Uruguay. A bit violent, but a masterpiece. It's very well filmed. It's sure to get an Oscar nomination."

It didn't take much more to arrange the meeting. The detective had decided to keep his possession of the video a strict secret, even from his friend, the loyal "Rabbit" Vergara. He was considering alternatives with the time bomb he had in his hands but had yet to discern the best move. On one hand, he wasn't sure what he would tell Sofía. On the other, he knew that if he stirred up the hornet's nest, she would suffer the consequences of a scandal in the press. This dichotomy was tearing him apart. The temptation to send Bonilla to rot in jail was hard to resist. Upon arriving at the club, the detective picked up the admission pass the lieutenant colonel had left for him at reception. Following the directions given by an employee, he headed toward the two distant figures, situated beyond the verdant Paspalum, under the grove. He wasn't worried about going alone; he knew Bonilla wouldn't try anything in a public place. The park's splendor no longer captivated him as it had the first and only time, he had visited it with Sofía. He remembered the picnic under the eucalyptus trees. Lying on their backs, they looked up at the cloud-washed sky. She rested her head on his shoulder. They both dreamed of an idyllic future in the United States. He refocused on his objective. Now he was walking on the grass to meet one of the most despicable beings the dictatorship had produced. Bonilla remained with his hand extended when the detective stood before him. He raised his eyebrows suspiciously, erased the smile he had started, and put his hand back in his pocket. Adrián took out a cigar and held it in his mouth. Before lighting it, he looked over the caddie who had stopped a few meters behind Bonilla. The dark-skinned man had a dim-witted face with a hairy wart at the corner of his lip. He was left-handed, the detective noted, with his hand hidden inside the right side of his jacket, at torso height, while he watched him intently.

"What are you looking at, faggot? If you're a caddie, I'm Gardel," Adrián snapped, twisting his mouth. "Take your hand off the gun, you dumb soldier. Go sit in the shade of the cypresses until I finish talking to your boss."

The other man raised his eyebrows, tightened his lips; he made a move to advance but stopped when Bonilla turned his head.

"Go on, Luisito," the military man said, nodding towards the grove. Out of professional habit, Luisito almost saluted his superior but remembered that morning he was a caddie and stopped his hand midway. A mocking snort escaped Adrián's mouth at the subordinate's clumsiness.

"I want to clarify one thing, my friend," Bonilla began to say, his tone conciliatory. "If you think I have something to do with Carlota's murder because she appears in the video, you're wrong."

Adrián merely exhaled the smoke and slightly raised his chin. He said nothing. Bonilla felt the icy stare: he endured it for a few seconds until his pupils burned. He blinked, looked up at the sky, and added: "I don't deny that I would have eliminated her if I had known she had the video that incriminated me, but I have nothing to do with that woman's death."

The argument was coherent. Adrián's instinct told him that Bonilla probably wasn't the murderer. Otherwise, he would have killed not only Carlota but also her son. He had another reason for confronting the military man: to stir the waters and see what surfaced.

"She must have stolen it from the basement library, the treacherous bitch. Sooner or later, women always screw you," Bonilla said loudly, but speaking to himself. "She thought she could blackmail me by giving it to the families of all those commies we had to eliminate to cleanse the nation," he concluded with a tone bordering on the solemn.

A crooked smile began to form on the detective's face.

"Don't go on, or you'll make me cry," he said mockingly, tilting his head back slightly. "All that's missing is for you to sing the national anthem."

Bonilla's expression changed for a moment, but he quickly reacted with a smile and raised his hands as if resigned to the lack of understanding.

"And Lucrecia Contreras, why did you kill her?" Adrián continued. "Was she getting too close to the truth with the mothers of the disappeared?"

"Who?" the military man reacted, raising his voice a little.

"The one-armed woman who ended up with her neck crushed in the Palacio Salvo. Does that ring a bell?"

"Look, sir . . ." Bonilla said, taking a step forward in an attempt to touch the detective's arm affably, convincingly. The detective stepped back without taking his eyes off him. "I swear on my children that I have nothing to do with that death. I know that after seeing the video, you think I'm despicable, but those were very hard times! We had to rid the nation of the red plague spreading across Latin America. I don't deny that we tortured to discover the whereabouts of the Tupamaros, but I've been retired from all that violence for years." He paused, clasped his hands in a pleading gesture, and continued in a low, conciliatory tone. "You must give me any copies of the tape. Let's be frank. It would cause your client great pain to know that her sister witnessed what we did. No one would gain anything."

"The mothers of the disappeared would gain," Adrián said, "when they learned that their children's murderer ended up with his ass violated in the penitentiary before having his throat cut."

Bonilla's pupils flared, but years of training masked his intentions, allowing him to dampen his anger. He knew he had a dog ready to bite in front of him.

"Can you imagine the pain it would cause the sister if you published that?" Bonilla insisted.

Adrián retracted the right corner of his lip toward his cheek, forming a dimple.

"What sensitivity to empathize with others! You devoted yourself altruistically to torturing, raping pregnant women, giving newborns to infertile couples, and throwing their mothers, alive, from a plane into the waters of the Río de la Plata. And as if that wasn't enough, you now worry about my client's feelings. What a noble soul you are, sir!" Adrián said, ending the last sentence with a soft, almost inaudible applause. "You are an unrecognized hero. A life dedicated to the well-being of your compatriots."

Bonilla raised his chin in response to the expression of disgust on the detective's face.

"Let's do this, my dear José Gervasio Artigas," the detective continued. "I'll pretend to believe that you didn't send Carlota to her grave and that Mother Teresa gave birth to you, but to get the video, you'll have to anonymously donate three hundred thousand greenbacks to the FAPEHD."

"The what?" Bonilla reacted, tensing all the muscles and features of his face.

"Educational Aid Fund for the Children of the Disappeared, my dear lieutenant colonel," Adrián clarified. "In other words, all those kids you left orphaned. They are now in the care of their grandparents, who must provide food, health, and education for their grandchildren with their meager pensions."

"Let's be reasonable, Fontana. Where am I going to get that fortune? You're delusional."

"You have plenty of contacts to request a loan against your house in Punta del Este. The truth is, I don't care how you get it. I'll give you a month. Once the donation is made, you'll have the video in your hands."

"And who assures me you won't betray me?"

"There's no such thing as a sure thing, my dear lieutenant colonel. The risk is your problem."

"If I don't get the money and you give the tape to the press, I insist it will be your client who suffers the consequences of your lack of foresight."

"The sister's feelings mean nothing to me. I'm paid to find the culprit. Spare me all that emotional crap about how my client would feel knowing that Carlota watched you fry your victims' balls," the detective said. He ended his argument by crushing the cigarette between his thumb and index finger and flicking it towards Bonilla's feet. Then he gave an informal salute, quickly touching his forehead with his fingers, turned around, and walked away.

Although he was certain he wouldn't reveal the tape to the press, he hoped the bluff had sounded convincing. The makeshift caddie, who had been leaning against the trunk of an ombú tree with his arms crossed, straightened up quickly. He looked for a sign on his boss's face, an indication to take action. Bonilla squinted his eyes and shook his head in disapproval. He probably doubted his lackey was a worthy opponent for the detective. For now, that was how things stood. The military man knew he had a month to weigh his options.

# XXV

ADRIÁN TOOK THE LAST sip of scotch and ordered another. It was around noon, and the kitchen at Yoruga was already in full swing. He glanced at his watch. "Rabbit" Vergara was late. Adrián wanted to know the details of the autopsy, but he knew Commissioner Bermúdez would object. To anticipate the circumstances, he had turned to his friend. Rabbit's connections inside and outside the Montevideo police headquarters might allow him to access the forensic analysis. What did the bloodied scraps of skin clinging to Lucrecia Contreras's nails reveal? At first, Rabbit had flatly refused to bribe the doctor to obtain a copy of the autopsy. In the end, Adrián had his way.

"This is the last favor I do for you, Fontana," Rabbit had said.

"Agreed, Vergara, the last one, I swear on the light that guides me," Adrián had promised.

"Damn it! You're going to get me locked up or dumped in a ditch," Rabbit had muttered as he left.

The waiter placed the glass of scotch on the table and added a small plate with pieces of bread, cheese, and chopped sausage, all held together with toothpicks.

"The appetizer is on the house," the server clarified.

Adrián winked and raised his fist with his thumb extended upwards. As he was about to eat a slice of sausage, a Manila envelope landed on the table.

"Here you go!" said Rabbit. "It took a lot of convincing for the forensic doctor. He finally caved like a whore when I showed him the greenbacks. You owe me 250 dollars."

"Good job, Rabbit. I knew I could count on you. Can I pay you with fennel or carrots? Sometimes bartering is more convenient than cash."

"Stop joking and read, you fool!" said Rabbit while nibbling on a piece of cheese. "And order me a glass of whiskey; my throat is dry from all the chatter with the forensic doctor."

Adrián turned his head and signaled to the counter. After the waiter took the order, he started pulling the report out of the envelope. He read it carefully. Then, he looked up over his glasses.

"But it says here that there were traces of . . . Did you discuss it with him?"

"Exactly," said Rabbit, nodding as well. "There were traces of saltpeter and sand in the groove in the neck that cut off the victim's air," he added, mimicking what had come out of the forensic doctor's mouth with such firmness that it gave the impression the diagnosis was his.

"And the nails? Any indication of DNA from the skin beneath them?" Adrián asked, impatient.

"Everything suggests that the epidermis belongs to the killer. Lucrecia must have scratched him while fighting him," said Rabbit, still immersed in a role that led him to bite his lower lip and squint as if engaged in a serious exercise of mental acuity.

The detective found it amusing that Rabbit had become so technical, so formal as to say "epidermis," and he let out a snort.

"Come on, Sherlock Holmes, what else did the doctor tell you?"

"According to the expert," Rabbit continued, "the strangulation could have been done with a nylon fishing line, judging by the depth of the groove in the flesh and the particles of sand and saltpeter."

He paused and used the plural to remain immersed in his fantasy.

"We speculate that the killer might have used a thick fishing line, like the one used at the end of the line to reinforce the pull of the sinker. Do you understand?"

"A fisherman . . ." Adrián said, his gaze lost. "A fisherman . . ." he repeated as he slowly stood up, in slow motion, absorbed in his thoughts. After a few seconds, he snapped out of his daze and kissed the top of his friend's head, who was looking at him with lips forming a capital "O."

"You're a genius, dear Rabbit! If you were a woman, I'd kiss you on the mouth."

He grabbed the jacket hanging on the back of the chair, quickly pulled out some dollars from his wallet, and handed them to Rabbit.

"Here, pay the bill. I'll call you later," he concluded as he headed for the exit.

"But where are you going, brother?" Rabbit inquired,

raising his arms. Adrián had already crossed the door and was running towards his car.

When the waiter arrived with the whiskey, Rabbit ordered a rib-eye steak with a side of fries. The mystery of what was going through Adrián's mind had made him hungry.

# XXVI

A FEW HOURS AFTER his conversation with Rabbit, Adrián met Juana at Café Martínez. As usual, he had seated himself by one of the windows, the most secluded in the room. Juana was sitting with her back to the crowd, and Adrián facing the door to keep a good watch on who entered the café. He never let his guard down. He knew he had made too many enemies in his short stay in Montevideo.

They had ordered a long cappuccino for him and a tea with milk accompanied by pastaflora for her, specially recommended by the waiter.

"Tell me more about the day you saw Consuelo with a fisherman on the rambla," Adrián said while she dipped the tea bag in the cup and covered it with the saucer.

"I don't know . . . he was an ordinary guy. I didn't see his face. They were both sitting with their backs to us, on the rambla wall with their feet dangling towards the water. He held the fishing rod in his right hand and embraced her around the waist with his left. She was leaning on his shoulder," Juana said, raising her eyebrows listlessly.

She still had a distant look, her eyes shadowed by dark bags that accentuated her weary expression. Along with her comrade in grief, the hope of finding her son's body had vanished.

"What else? Do you remember if he was tall, fat, thin?" he asked softly, controlling his impatience.

Juana closed her eyes as if to force the memory.

"He was kind of bald and had an egg-shaped head."

"What else, Juana, what else?"

Exhausted by the limits of her memory, the driver raised her eyebrows and shook her head.

"Relax, Juana. Don't worry. You're still dazed by the pain. Come on, drink your tea before it gets cold and dig into that pastaflora before I eat it myself. It looks amazing!" he said, smiling.

"We'll share it, Adrián," she said, grabbing the knife to divide the portion.

"No, no, go ahead, just take a bite. I don't eat at this hour."

Juana complied. They sat in silence for a few minutes. She leaned her elbow on the table, holding her head, while she chewed slowly. The detective lit a cigarette and looked out the window. The waning autumn sun struggled to filter through the foliage of the plane trees and landed with pale afternoon light on the sidewalk. Dark gray clouds loomed ominously behind them, heralding the storm the TV behind the bar counter had announced.

Suddenly, Juana slammed her palm on the table, spilling tea over the edges of the cup. Excited, she looked at her interlocutor as if enlightened by the Holy Spirit.

"The tattoo!" she exclaimed. "When he was hugging the maid, I saw a black rose tattooed on his left forearm!"

Adrián froze for a moment. His memory sparked reflexively. The tattoo. An image consistent with the paradox of why our vision archives the significant and the trivial in the neurons of the subconscious. And suddenly, there it was again, the flash. The rose tattoo, vivid and clear before his retina.

"Are you sure?" he asked fervently, leaning forward and placing his hands on the table.

"Yes, yes, absolutely sure. He had a black rose tattooed on his forearm!"

Adrián stretched across the table and gave her a loud kiss on the forehead. He stood up and grabbed the driver's head in his hands.

"You're worth your weight in gold, big girl!" he said, putting on his jacket as he left. As he reached the exit, he turned around. "You'd better head home. The storm is coming."

She tried to mumble something, asking him to explain, but Adrián had already disappeared through the door of the Yoruga.

# XXVII

Sharp as a violin, the whistle of the south wind came from the sea and ascended the steep streets that led to the rambla, as if it were providing background music for an uncertainty. A future drama, suspense galloping bareback in the storm. The monumental force of nature unleashed over Punta Carretas. The Río de la Plata had stretched to the seawall of the rambla with overwhelming, apocalyptic arrogance. The surge boiled with foam on the crest of the waves and roared as it approached the coast, like a monster drooling with rabid saliva. The short-interval waves clapped hysterically and incessantly against the rocks. They soared gracefully over the edge of the granite wall and transformed into a final whirlpool of air and water that ended up shattering on the asphalt of the highway.

There was not a soul on the street. The brutal storm had been announced. Meteorologists had warned of the possibility of flooding, and the residents of Montevideo had hurried to shelter in their homes after leaving work. The night was not fit for happy hour outings or gatherings with friends in the bars of Pocitos.

Alonso, sitting in the lobby, was barely distinguishable through the rain-soaked glass of the entrance. He folded the evening paper he had in his hands, put his glasses in the outer pocket of his jacket, and checked the time. It was eight forty. He still had twenty minutes to finish his workday.

The doorman stood up, clasped his hands behind his back, and walked to the opposite end of the hall to stretch his legs. When he turned around, he saw a male silhouette watching him, standing at the entrance with legs slightly apart. A strange premonition, like the sixth sense of animals when they smell danger, ran through his spine. The shadow dripped water from the plastic hood covering most of his face.

The doorman took his bifocals out of his blazer pocket again to see better as he approached the entrance. He opened it a few centimeters, cautiously, placing one foot behind the door. When the stranger pulled down his hood, the doorman raised his eyebrows and widened his egg-shaped eyes even more.

"Mr. Fontana, you gave me quite a scare! You look like you came straight from hell," he said with a smile that failed to camouflage the pallor that invaded his face. "What are you doing here at this hour, in this crazy weather?"

"I have something very important to ask you for the case investigation," said Adrián, expressionless, his pupils contracted to tiny points.

Alonso's eyes acquired an indecipherable gleam. He blinked twice.

"Why don't you come by early tomorrow?" he said with a slight tremor in his lips. "I'm almost done. It's late, and I'm longing to rest. Come by tomorrow at nine, and I'll be happy to help you," he concluded, as he began to close the door.

Adrián placed his shoe between the opening and the frame.

"No, it can't wait. It must be now. It's very important," he replied, while his hand, lightly but firmly placed on the glass frame, overcame Alonso's resistance. The doorman stepped back in the face of the detective's six-foot frame, who was almost entirely inside the hall. He retreated further to better negotiate the height difference, visibly impatient, resigned to the invasion of his territory.

"Well, what's it about? Tell me."

"It's better if we discuss it in your room. It's delicate, and someone could overhear us here in the hall."

Alonso argued that his room was messy, and he was embarrassed. He insisted he was tired and that whatever the detective had to ask him, he would surely remember better the next day with a fresh mind. The detective didn't relent until he was behind the doorman as he unlocked the apartment door. It was in the building's basement. A hermetic, reinforced concrete basement. Gloomy, dark, full of pipes emitting unsettling sounds. It was like a bunker impenetrable by sunlight. It had no windows facing the street and didn't allow any sound from the surface to be heard.

"Come in, sit down," said the doorman, as he hung his jacket on the coat rack. "Would you like a little grappa? I always have one before dinner," he added, pointing to a bottle of honey grappa on a shelf in the living room.

"No, I'm fine," said Adrián, meanwhile surveying the stained and filthy studio apartment but never losing sight of the doorman's movements. An indecent mountain of plates with food remnants piled up in the kitchen sink.

A repugnant stench of confinement, stale air, and black mold prevailed in the hovel. All mixed with the smell of burnt coffee and tobacco. The same stench emanated from the doorman's body the first time he met him. The absence of windows increased the sense of claustrophobia. The decoration was minimal and in poor taste. A square, laminated Formica table with edges peeling off and rusty iron legs, with two matching chairs, served as a dining table. The cracked armchair Adrián sat on emitted a cigarette smell that clung to his clothes. But the most interesting thing was hanging on the wall next to the bathroom door. There, the doorman had four fiberglass fishing rods, medium and long-distance, equipped with reels, lines, and hooks, ready for fishing. Completing the arsenal were three wooden tackle boxes, a cast net, and several leaders arranged in line, from thicker to thinner lines, hanging on C-shaped hooks. Below, on the floor, was a bucket full of rags and a pair of gloves pressed against the handle.

"Are you a fishing enthusiast, Alonso?"

"Yes," replied the doorman, already returning with a glass of honey grappa in his hand. "It's a pleasure I indulge in, you know. It entertains me. It's a way to kill time on Sundays when I escape from this confinement to breathe some fresh air," he said, now more relaxed.

Adrián knew quite a bit about fishing terminology but asked with his best stupid face while approaching the wall.

"What a thickness of that line you have wrapped on the reel, Alonso. Is it for catching whales?"

The jocular comment served its intended effect. Alonso showed a faint smile without parting his lips. He placed the grappa glass on the table and approached the wall. He took down a tackle box and unrolled it to the point where the fine fishing line joined the thicker one. The doorman explained in an almost paternal tone:

"This is what fishermen call the leader, Mr. Fontana."

"And what's it for?"

"This goes at the end of the line and is thicker to withstand the impact of casting. It prevents the sinker from breaking the line. Understand?"

Adrián estimated it to be about a millimeter and a half in diameter.

"Look at that, how interesting. And it holds up well despite being nylon?"

Alonso let out a complacent chuckle.

"It doesn't break, my friend," he said condescendingly. "This line is strong enough to catch an 50-pound fish," he indicated, while tightening the leader between his fists.

Adrián took the fifty centimeters of nylon from Alonso's hands and stretched it too to test the tension.

"Look at that," he said pensively, head down for a moment, "you learn something new every day. So, it's strong enough to twist a person's neck?"

He kept his head down for a fraction of a second and then quickly lifted it to meet the doorman's eyes, certain his expression had changed. They stared at each other intently. Alonso's pupils now had the gleam of a cornered wild beast. A frozen snake contained, about to strike. He didn't have time. Adrián delivered a brutal elbow that hit between his nose and mouth. Something cracked behind the impact area. Alonso's body staggered backward as he grabbed his face with his hands. Blood began to seep through his fingers. A tooth dangled from a thread of bloody pulp above his lower lip. He let out a demonic scream and raised his arms towards his attacker, but it was too late for a second time. In a swift move, as quick as a feline, Adrián slipped behind him and tightened the leader around his neck. The doorman made a choking sound. He flailed desperately; his face filled with anguish.

"Let's see how you like a taste of your own medicine," Adrián said through gritted teeth. He twisted the wooden tackle to increase the pressure of the leader on the doorman's neck. The line began to sink into the fine groove carved in the skin by the twisting tourniquet.

Alonso spat up and tried to grasp the nylon slipping deeper and deeper into his skin. It was in vain. Adrián kept twisting the handle over the cord. Alonso's eyes threatened to pop out of their sockets. When he almost felt his life fading, the pressure ceased. He collapsed to the floor and writhed, his body contorting like the worms he cut in half to use as bait. Adrián walked beside him. Face down, Alonso gasped. His chest was a mad machine, revved up, trying to pump air that didn't come. It took him several minutes to slow his heartbeat and regain control of his lungs. He let out a compressed groan, already without strength, when the detective resumed action and yanked him by the hair. Adrián flipped him over on the floor. He placed his size 12 moccasin on Alonso's carotid and began to press.

"Now you're going to tell me everything, you miserable wretch, or I'll break your neck."

Alonso raised his clenched hands. In intervals, with a broken voice, entangled in an agony of coughs, cries, phlegm, and blood still dripping from his mouth, he promised he would talk.

# XXVIII

"Mrs. Carlota was hysterical. Her screams could be heard from the hallway. We also heard Javier's voice. She was accusing him of immorality for trying to blackmail her. He asked her if she wasn't disgusted by witnessing the tortures or being a whore and rolling around with Stern. 'You embarrass me with my friends and my girlfriend!' he said. Then they stopped shouting. We heard furniture being dragged, glass shattering against the wall. Consuelo and I remained silent in the hall. I always accompanied her to the apartment door. I suggested we leave, but she refused. She turned the key in the service entrance, which connects to the penthouse kitchen. I tried to stop her, but she put her finger on my lips. I feared for her safety. I peeked through the slightly open door."

Alonso paused to catch his breath and asked for a glass of water.

"Come on, keep going!" was the detective's response, accompanied by a slap to the face.

"Mrs. Carlota . . ." the doorman continued, stammering, rubbing his cheek, "seemed to be throwing everything she had at hand in the direction of her son. Suddenly, he stormed out. I was lucky he went the other way, towards the elevator. Otherwise, he would have seen me. He turned at the end of the hallway, and hearing the elevator doors open, I decided to enter the kitchen. Mrs. Carlota was now yelling at Consuelo."

Adrián found it comical and pathetic that the killer referred to his victim with the respectful "Mrs."

Then Alonso said something that left him frozen. For a moment, he thought he had misheard.

"What did you say, you bastard?"

Alonso hesitated, wondering if repeating it would earn him another blow. But the temptation was too strong.

"You heard right, Fontana! Mrs. Carlota told Consuelo that Javier's father was his grandfather. Yes, sir, the very same Don Ferraro! How do you think her sister will react if she finds out?" said the doorman, defiantly, with his chin held high.

Adrián gritted his teeth, grabbed him by the hair, and punched him in the mouth again. The doorman fell backward, laughing hysterically. He licked the blood from his lip as if savoring the taste of the blows.

"Yes, just as you heard, my dear Mr. Fontana. Incest! A paragon of virtue, the esteemed Don Ferraro."

Adrián hit him again with sadism, with rage, with frustration. He wasn't sure if he was doing it because Alonso might be lying to play with his mind or because, reading the doorman's eyes, an inner voice told him he was telling a horrible truth. A dark, nauseating secret, hidden from the world's eyes. He beat Alonso's face and thought of Sofía. Despite all her disagreements with her father, he knew that deep down, Sofía had always respected him.

Alonso couldn't take the beating any longer and went from laughter to tears.

"That's the pure truth, I swear! Stop hitting me! Ask Consuelo if you don't believe me. Mrs. Carlota was shouting at Consuelo that 'telling that bastard from hell who his real father was would be her perfect revenge.' She would humiliate him with his friends, with his fiancée. She would destroy his life. Consuelo was begging her not to make Javier suffer. She loves him as if he were her own son. She's obsessed with that little bastard. She'd do anything for him."

"How touching. Go on, filth, keep going!"

"Consuelo kept pleading for Javier. Then, Mrs. Carlota changed her posture. She became expressionless, like an automaton, isolated from Consuelo's presence. 'It's over!' she said when she snapped out of the trance. 'I'll call Stern, tell him everything, and ask him to give him a beating. That's the end for that son of a bitch!' Consuelo knew Stern was a cruel man. She feared for Javier's life. She begged again. Mrs. Carlota sat on the couch and started dialing. Consuelo lunged at her. They fell and rolled on the floor. They scratched; they fought like wild cats. Consuelo is younger, but Mrs. Carlota . . ."

"Stop calling her Mrs., idiot!" Adrián interrupted.

" . . . Carlota was a demon when she got angry. She got on top of my poor Consuelo and started beating her viciously."

"And then you came in with the nylon leader," said the detective.

"I wasn't going to let her get hurt. I pulled out the leader I kept in my pants pocket. I always carry one with me to make rigs while I'm on duty. I squeezed and squeezed until everything was calm and silent. A relief," Alonso said, fixated on that final word.

Sitting on the floor, exhausted and with his shoulders slumped, the doorman lowered his head and fell silent. After a few seconds, he looked at Adrián again. A sinister change in his face erased his previous tragic anti-hero posture, sacrificed for his beloved. He drew a crooked smile, a grimace accompanied by a diabolical turbulence in his pupils.

"No, my dear sir," he said, clicking his tongue three times in disapproval. "You can't hand me over to the police. Consuelo told me how much you love Sofía. Can you imagine how that poor little dove will suffer if she finds out that her respectable father had sex with her sister? If they arrest me, I swear I'll call her from prison and let her know. You'd better let me go. It's best for everyone. It will destroy your beloved's life. For the second time . . . as I understand."

Adrián looked at him intently. He toyed with the temptation to rip out all his teeth like a medieval dentist, without anesthesia. A sudden thought, an alternative option, flickered in his mind. He stepped back a few meters, pulled out his cell phone without taking his eyes off the killer, and started dialing. After a few seconds, he murmured a few brief words in English, unintelligible to Alonso. He hung up and put the phone back in his jacket pocket. He lit a cigarette and walked towards the doorman. He was still sitting on the floor, studying him. The detective kicked him in the chest. Alonso's body sprawled backward. He barely lifted his head and studied Adrián's eyes, trying to discern if he was going to kill him.

"Stay put and look at the ceiling until the police arrive. If you say half a word I don't like, I swear on my mother I'll start stomping on your face."

Alonso's facial expression confirmed he took the detective's threat seriously.

They remained still for a while. Alonso lay silent, eyes fixed on the ceiling, and Adrián sat in the armchair in front of him. He smoked cigarettes like a chain smoker, weighing the decision he had made. He morbidly threw a still-lit cigarette butt onto the doorman's body. He squirmed like a reptile to shake it off and cursed with his eyes.

"And why did you kill Lucrecia, you piece of shit?" Adrián said. He stretched out his leg and kicked Alonso in the ribs.

The doorman howled and crawled further back. He leaned his back against the wall and spoke calmly, void of emotion.

"That one-armed woman was snooping around too much. She told me she had seen us together on the boardwalk. She was obsessed with the idea that we were accomplices in Carlota's murder. She sent someone to follow us. I noticed the second time I saw him when he sat next to us on the Sarandí street pier to listen to our conversation. I remembered his gaunt face with a parrot-beak nose."

"Was it this guy?" Adrián said, approaching the doorman to show him the photo on his phone screen.

"Yes, that skinny bastard," confirmed the doorman with a smile.

The one-armed woman covered all angles, thought Adrián. She used the same fool to follow not only the doorman but also him. To see who would first serve her the whereabouts of the white wolf on a silver platter.

"We were sitting on the pier wall," Alonso continued. "I mentioned to Consuelo that you had asked me about the white wolf painting. I asked her if she knew where it was. She said no, but she had heard the one-armed woman tell Carlota that it was worth a fortune. Then I realized Consuelo had spoken too loudly. I looked to the side and recognized the parrot-beak face. He had heard everything. I said goodbye to Consuelo and followed him. Now I would be the spy. I saw him enter the Palacio Salvo. He took the elevator to the seventeenth floor. I looked at the nameplate to see who lived there. Lucrecia Contreras. I left and told Consuelo. The next day, the one-armed woman called me. She wanted to meet with us to talk about the painting or she would go to the police and accuse us of the murder. I don't think she had proof, but after receiving the spy's report, she suspected we had killed Carlota and maybe the painting was in our possession. She proposed a meeting at the Salvo at half past nine. I wasn't born yesterday. I went three hours earlier and killed her."

That seemed to explain why Lucrecia had set the meeting with him at half-past eight, Adrián thought. An hour before the meeting with Alonso. She counted on him forcing the doorman to confess to the crime.

"The one-armed woman was playing poker with us," Alonso continued. "She couldn't know we had killed Carlota. Otherwise, she wouldn't have waited so long to contact us. She was guided by intuition. She had a very developed sixth sense, that dyke. Her talent cost her dearly, hehehe," he said, his eyes brimming with perverse pleasure. "Consuelo asked me not to kill her. I didn't listen. Leaving her alive was too big a risk. Sooner or later the police would be on our trail."

"And the skinny guy who followed you? He could also compromise you."

"I planned to take care of him today, but the storm ruined my plans. I'll have to postpone it until tomorrow," he said, with a malicious smile.

The doorman tried to sit up.

"Go on, coward, keep talking," Adrián said, discouraging the attempt with another kick to the ribs. "How did you kill her?"

"I went to the Palacio Salvo and went up to the 17th floor. It wasn't difficult to pick the lock. I used to be a locksmith before working as a doorman. The one-armed woman came in from the street, made herself a drink, and sat down to watch TV in the living room. I approached from behind with the fishing leader.

I never thought she could resist with such energy. Just one arm and she fought like she had three," he concluded with a laugh. The temptation to taunt the detective was stronger than his survival instinct.

Adrián sprang up from the armchair like a spring. Ready to stomp him like a cockroach. A pulp without a trace of humanity smashed against the floor. He was advancing towards the doorman when the door opened. The imposing figures of "Cheeks" Stern and King Kong entered the room.

"That's enough, Fontana. We'll take it from here," Stern said. He was a quick reader and deduced that Adrián was about to spoil his taste for revenge.

King Kong grabbed the doorman by the clothes and lifted him into the air as if he were a child.

"What are they doing here?" Alonso exclaimed, kicking without touching the floor. He recognized Carlota's boyfriend. "I want to surrender to the police!"

King Kong clamped half his face with his massive hand. Alonso stopped shouting and looked at him in terror. The perverse pleasure and suicidal impulse had completely dissipated, now clear of a horrible end, a long agony before the final blow. All of Montevideo knew of Stern's unlimited sadism, and he was no exception. He was in the hands of a butcher who would be very creative in settling accounts with his girlfriend's killer. He remained suspended in the air, pinned by the gorilla's enormous arms. A yellowish liquid slid down his pants and dripped onto the body-guard's feet.

"You pissed yourself, dumbass!" King Kong reacted. He threw him against the wall with a gesture like throwing a sack of potatoes.

Stern let out a muffled laugh.

Adrián put on his raincoat and headed for the door. As he passed by Stern, the latter elbowed his arm.

"I won't forget this, Mike Hammer. I owe you one," said Cheeks.

Adrián looked at him but said nothing.

"Thanks for the heads-up," Stern added, winking.

The detective opened the door and walked slowly down the basement hallway. When he reached the stairs leading to the main floor, he could still hear the almost inaudible echo of Alonso's pleas. A distant sound, inconsequential for the reinforced basement walls.

He stepped out onto the boardwalk. The rain was still pouring down. He didn't put on his hood. He let the fever and filth that had clung to his body and soul wash away.

It was almost midnight. He vanished into the storm of water and wind just as he had arrived. An apparition from hell, according to the doorman's words. Or Michael . . . the warrior angel of God. That's what Juana would have called him if she had believed in divine justice.

# XXIX

Rabbit was already aware of the latest events. He was the only one with whom Adrián had decided to share the sordid details behind the crime: the video of the tortures, the incest, and his decision to leave the doorman in Stern's hands. The detective firmly believed that a secret was not truly a secret if two people knew it, but he had no other alternative. He needed his help. Rabbit had always shown him impeccable loyalty. Despite this, Adrián took Rabbit's large face firmly in his hands to emphasize that the truth must never reach Sofía's ears. The fact that "Cheeks" Stern was involved guaranteed that Rabbit would be the most discreet of mortals.

It was eleven in the morning, and Adrián had been dialing the maid's number since eight, without any answer. He cursed the mistake he had made the previous night. Although he didn't know her address or that of the elderly woman, she cared for in Pocitos, he had assumed that having Consuelo's phone number was enough. It was almost certain that she would answer. He wouldn't have been able to contact Alonso, and she wouldn't suspect anything. Hoping that the doorman was still alive, he decided to call Stern. He spoke in code to avoid compromising him. He asked him to get Consuelo's address.

"Everything's all sewn up," was Cheeks's response. Néstor Alonso was no longer among the living. For a moment, he felt his hands stained with blood. When the image of the doorman blackmailing him with the incest came back to his mind, the feeling of guilt dissipated. Could Alonso have also killed Consuelo, and that's why she wasn't answering? Given the circumstances, that possibility didn't bother him. On the contrary, it was a relief. The ideal solution. The carnal stain of the food industry magnate, dead and buried. However, something told him it wouldn't be that easy. Perhaps during the storm over Montevideo,

Consuelo had gotten scared and called her boyfriend in the early morning, and not finding him, she might suspect something and decide to hide. "Only a bloody rookie forgets to ask for the accomplice's address in a murder!" he repeated to himself, looking in the mirror while waiting for Rabbit. He was tormented by the possibility that, cornered, Consuelo might decide to turn herself in to the police and confess everything. He also wasn't sure what he would do when he found her. Would he be capable of killing for Sofía? Of committing a crime to protect her? The ultimate proof of love and sacrifice that would cleanse his conscience. He briefly considered handing her over to Stern. No, no! he told himself, discarding the idea immediately. The thought repulsed him. After all, the poor wretch was a victim of the circumstances. She hadn't even been the murderous hand. It irritated him to realize that his mind was caught in a vicious circle, a frenzied madness. Alonso was different. A miserable being, an insignificant earthworm. Perhaps he could try to get her out of the country in exchange for her silence. "Rabbit knows a lot of people in Argentina and Brazil. He can help me if I ask him," he convinced himself as he got dressed.

He was still obsessing over all the angles when the phone rang, interrupting his thoughts. It was the receptionist. His friend was waiting for him in the lobby.

Adrián's throat was dry. Before leaving, he opened a bottle of Agua Salus and drank it to the last drop. He put on his suede jacket, left the room, and pressed the elevator button. As he descended, an idea occurred to him. Something only "Rabbit" Vergara could manage.

Seated behind the wheel, Rabbit scratched his chin. He was weighing his friend's question. It was a very good option. Did he know anyone in the public utilities' services, water, electricity, or gas? Someone who could quickly provide the address of a woman named Consuelo Flores. He scratched his neck and dived into the vast database stored in his memory. After a moment, his eyes lit up. He opened the contact list on his phone and pressed the letter L.

"Here it is!" he murmured.

He dialed enthusiastically and after the "Hello, Lettuce, long time, brother!" and the rest of the protocol greetings, he explained the situation. "Lettuce" Martínez, who worked at O.S.E., the potable water supply company, told him he would call him back shortly. Fifteen minutes later, the answer came. There were three addresses with the same name and surname: Florería Consuelo Flores, Concepción Consuelo Flores, and just Consuelo Flores. The first was discarded without hesitation. Florería Consuelo Flores, the famous flower shop in Montevideo, undoubtedly had nothing to do with Carlota's maid. Concepción Consuelo Flores . . . ? Although it was possible that Consuelo had two names and preferred using the second, the detective left this option as a Plan B. The third lived in Euskal Erría 70, in Malvín Norte, and that's where Rabbit Vergara's car headed.

Malvín Norte was a middle to lower-middle-class neighborhood that until the early 1970s was mostly composed of small farms and country homes. Over time, it had become overcrowded with public housing complexes and housing cooperatives. Some streets with humble dwellings, mostly inhabited by retired elderly people, still survived. There were also cantegriles. This was what Uruguayans called the precarious settlements built on vacant lots, amid the trash.

The Euskal Erría 70, 71, and 92 complexes, all within the neighborhood, contained a total of six thousand homes.

Collectively, Euskal Erría was considered the largest building project in the country's history. It had developed in the 1980s. No one had ever been able to decipher why they had named it Erría without an H.

The area's reputation had greatly depreciated after November 22, 2004. Some boys aged between fifteen and twenty were celebrating a birthday in front of tower 30 of the Euskal Erría 70 complex. A police officer from the 222 service, special surveillance of the complex, approached the group who were peacefully chanting songs from different football fans. "I don't want to see you here, I'll kill you," he said as he passed by. After a while, the boys resumed the noise, but this time they included a classic football chant: "Porompompón, porompompón, the one who doesn't jump is a snitch." The uniformed officer, i.e., the "snitch," which along with the term "milico" are the two most derogatory forms Uruguayans use to refer to the police, confronted them again. This time pointing his regulation weapon at them. "Go ahead, shoot, cowardly milico," said Santiago Yerle, 18, probably convinced that the officer wouldn't fire. "Santi," as everyone in the neighborhood knew him, received a bullet in the leg and another in the chest. This is how the tragedy that ended with Yerle's death and five wounded was born. After this, the police insisted on labeling Malvín Norte as a red zone, although the statistics didn't show a very different crime profile from any other neighborhood in Montevideo. Later, with the arrival of crack cocaine, it also became one of the main drug distribution points in the metropolitan area. Improvised robberies, snatchings of old ladies' purses coming back from collecting their pensions, armed thefts in local businesses, rapes, stabbings. Everything contributed to the sense of insecurity that was felt in the neighborhood.

They parked the car at the corner of Yrigoyen and Iguá streets. Rabbit left his wallet under the floor mat and got ready to leave the car to accompany his friend. Adrián stopped him.

"Wait for me here, Vergara. If we both go, we'll find the Renault without wheels when we come back."

"Are you sure, brother? Be careful, look, in this neighborhood, they'll fuck you in the ass."

"That's why it's better if I go alone," Adrián said with a mocking smile. "If they rape your ass, you might end up liking it."

Rabbit shook his head and rolled his eyes. He got out of the car and opened the trunk.

"Here, take this," he said, handing him a crowbar. "It'll help you force the door if she doesn't open, or to crack the skull of a junkie who approaches you with bad intentions."

Adrián thought that the knife he kept inside his jacket was more than enough to deal with any lowlife that confronted him. In any case, he thought it was a good idea to take the crowbar to open Consuelo's door.

"Lock the doors, Vergara. Call me on the cell if anything happens."

It didn't take him long to find tower C. The signage was better than the bad image of the place. In a public phone booth, only the cable was hanging. Two dirty-faced kids with adult expressions were rummaging through a garbage container. The taller one displayed a smile of rotten teeth as he threw a found condom at his companion. The other dodged it and shouted, "Fuck your sister!" while wiping the green snot blocking his nostrils with the sleeve of his sweater. To complete the picture, they were accompanied by a mangy dog whose ribs could be counted.

Adrián took the elevator to the ninth floor. When he got off, he walked down a narrow, grimy-floored corridor, where a noticeable smell of frying lingered. The sticky walls showed the typical graffiti, common in a public bathroom. A gallery exhibiting the filth of improvised and twisted artists; hidden within anonymous drawings of explicit sex, and rhymed verses that induced fellatio, or dedicated to expose the homosexual condition of some guy who lived in the building.

He gave two short knocks on 903. He waited with his ear pressed to the door. Nothing. No sign of footsteps approaching. He tested the latch. He assessed the lock's resistance. Simple, without a security cylinder. A suicidal attitude in a neighborhood of that ilk. Apparently, Consuelo didn't invest much in preserving her life. It didn't take him much to break the fragile lock. The time was right not to alert any curious neighbor. Most would be working, he thought, given the reigning silence behind the doors.

The detective's radar scanned the apartment. Sobriety prevailed. A life marked by abstinence. In the living room, a black suede sofa, a TV, and a plywood table with four plastic chairs. The walls were sky blue, starting to peel, and devoid of decorations or ornaments. The exception was a photo of the maid with the boy Javier, an image of the Virgin Mary, and a calendar whose page hadn't been changed since the beginning of the year.

Adrián pushed open the bedroom door with his foot. The same minimalism. An iron enamel bed neatly made. Next to it, a nightstand and a small lamp made up the rest of the furniture. He turned on the light in the tiny bathroom and drew back the shower curtain.

The kitchen also had only the basics. An old fridge, a stove with spiral burners, and a Primus stove on the counter where a kettle rested. A thermos, mate, and straw. Two pots and a pan hung on a hook. Half a dozen glasses on a shelf. The sink was empty. Nothing to wash. Frugal, but neat, thought the detective. Nothing out of the ordinary. However, something caught his attention. On the counter was a grocery bag still unpacked. The tip of a French loaf, missing its end, protruded from inside. Adrián felt the baguette with his fingers and noticed it wasn't completely hard yet. Consuelo had to have been there the night before. He emptied the rest of the contents: a packet of Adria noodles, a can of tomato sauce, and a packet of grated cheese. At the bottom of the bag was the grocery receipt. He took out his reading glasses from his jacket. The receipt was dated the day before, and the printed time of issuance on the strip read six twenty in the evening, just before the storm that had hit Montevideo the previous night. If Consuelo had arrived at her apartment at the start of the storm, it was most likely that she hadn't left until the next morning. Where was she? Why wasn't she answering the phone? He reasoned that Alonso couldn't have killed her. The analysis of the times proved it. During the storm, Alonso was at the doorman's lodge, and what had happened afterward cleared him of suspicion. He pocketed the receipt and left the room.

As he approached the Renault, Rabbit was exhaling a puff through the small opening he had left in the window to let the smoke escape.

He got in and asked him to drive around the neighborhood a bit, just in case they saw her. They then decided to return to Pocitos to wander the streets. Somewhere in the maze of buildings of the crowded neighborhood lived the old woman Consuelo was taking care of. Finding the maid on the street, going to the pharmacy or the grocery store, was harder than trying to smoke underwater, but they had no other option. It was that or sitting at the Yoruga to let time pass, and Adrián at that moment had ants in his pants. He wanted to stay in motion.

As they circled the roundabout at Plaza Biarritz, Adrián startled his friend's calmness. Rabbit was holding the steering wheel with one hand and sipping a Diet Coke with a straw that he had bought at the drive-thru window of McDonald's.

"Fuck! Fuck! Fuck!" the detective cursed angrily, punching the glove compartment.

"Now what's the matter?" said Rabbit, lifting his lips from the straw.

"Sofía arrives in Montevideo next week! Damned luck!" Adrián replied, rolling his eyes and raising his head towards the car roof. His ex's message on the cellphone screen burned in his hands. She couldn't have picked a worse time, he thought. "Rabbit, we must find Consuelo before Sofía lands in Carrasco."

# XXX

NIGHT FALLS IN POCITOS. Adrián argues on the phone. He frowns, his mouth twists with contempt. On the other end, Bonilla tries to persuade him that he needs three months to get the money. "You have thirteen days left. Once the deadline passes, I will make the video public," says the detective, hanging up abruptly.

He knows that the ex-executioner of Operation Condor has plenty of cold blood and is only trying to buy time. The detective's life insurance rests on the lie that Bonilla has believed: a friend possesses copies of the video abroad. But he is also aware that with a criminal of that caliber, nothing is predictable. If the military man asks for an extension, it's certainly not to donate a cent to FAPEHD. This doesn't keep Adrián up at night. He limits himself to staying alert and not slacking off with the bluffing. After hanging up, he smiles, imagining Bonilla's curse on the other end of the line.

That morning, Sofía had arrived in Montevideo. Adrián had asked "Rabbit" Vergara to pick her up at the airport while he made another round through the Euskal Erría Complex. His obsession is to locate Consuelo. He is terrified by the possibility that, feeling cornered, in a moment of rage or madness, she might contact Sofía and tell her everything. But it has been in vain. The apartment was the same. Everything in its place. It's a miracle that thieves haven't emptied it. Sometimes in the worst neighborhoods, an unlocked door goes unnoticed and is safer than a thousand locks. He hasn't asked anything of the neighbors or the nearby store. They could tip her off. It was also likely that she had sought refuge in Aguas Quietas, her hometown. Last week he traveled with Rabbit to discreetly ask for help from the town's sheriff, the father-in-law of a smuggler who supplies whisky to his friend. They turned the town upside down. They visited four out of five families named Flores, residing in Aguas Quietas. Consuelo's was the only one left, but the neighbors informed them that her parents had died long ago, and her siblings emigrated to Brazil. Could she have gone in search of her family and crossed the border? His instinct told him that she remained in Montevideo, to be close to Javier.

It's already seven-fifteen, and he had agreed with Sofía to have dinner together at the Victoria Plaza restaurant. Now that he's shaken off Bonilla's call, he undresses and showers. Then he chooses clothes that aren't too worn and leaves his room. While waiting for the elevator, he smooths out the wrinkles in his pants with his hand in front of the hall mirror. He checks his wristwatch. He has twenty minutes to get to downtown.

The Victoria Plaza Hotel has shared Plaza Independencia since 1952 with other historical icons of classic Montevideo: the Palacio Salvo, the Ciudadela Gate, and the Government House. All situated around the landscaped quadrangle at the center of which stands the enormous equestrian statue of the national hero. The legendary Don José Gervasio Artigas, who had inspired Adrián's cynicism by comparing him to Bonilla. Fifty meters further back is the Solís Theater, and the distinguished restaurant El Águila, frequented by the crème de la crème of Uruguayan society. It's a privileged location for those who want to soak up the Montevideo of yesteryear. Here also begins 18 de Julio Avenue, and at the opposite end, the Old City, The Cabildo, and the Matriz Church. For several decades the hotel had been the only five-star in the capital and had hosted most of the heads of state who visited the country.

Before entering the luxurious entrance hall, Adrián extinguishes his cigarette in the ornate bronze ashtray by the revolving door. At the reception, he announces his appointment to a young man with a stiff posture. He sits down to wait for his ex-girlfriend in a perfectly cushioned red velvet armchair. Minutes later, Sofía emerges from the elevator wrapped in a halo of splendor that immediately captivates the gaze of both sexes. There's something for everyone. Fifty-somethings with drooling irises or young men carrying a libido that threatens to overflow through their pupils. Some young women scrutinize her from head to toe with eyes filled with comparative jealousy. More mature women watch in awe. The detective is amused to see the bellboy almost bump into a guest while ogling Sofía's rear. He's also entertained by an elderly foreign-looking man who receives a pinch on his arm from his wife. "Have you lost something?" she asks, seeing her husband's persistence in turning around with dazed eyes.

The beautiful woman with whom he shared the best years of his life is wearing a sapphire blue dress that ends midway down her well-proportioned thighs. Her naturally tanned arms are bare. The neckline shows just enough without being explicit. Her mane rests on her shoulders, tousled in innate curls. The kind that forms after a bath when she deliberately leaves her hair damp and shakes it with her hands, skipping the brush or blow dryer. A planned mess that Adrián, lying on the bed, had witnessed so many times with enchantment, while she got ready, back in the days of the northern hemisphere.

She has meticulously applied makeup with the precision of an artist to stretch the midtones. Purple and caramel shadows highlight her coffee-colored eyes. She has barely hinted at blush on her cheeks and has chosen a pure, vibrant red lipstick, going up, down, and up again over the gentle relief of the cupid's bow.

She walks towards him. She wears high heels and has serious, tempered irises. Adrián stands up. She stretches and kisses him on that indistinct border between the cheek and the corner of the lip. The detective's radar notices the unusual closeness but does not rule out that it's due to a miscalculation, given their height difference.

"Cabotin," she says with a mocking grimace. "As always, you're a copycat."

Adrián just smiles. He says nothing but is pleased that she noticed.

After ordering dinner, Sofía asks about the progress of the investigation. Adrián tells her that he suspects the building's doorman. "According to witnesses," he explains, "he's also a fisherman." He tells her the autopsy details. She listens calmly, professionally, as if it were one of her cases as a criminal lawyer.

"Did you interrogate him?"

"I couldn't find him. Apparently, he's on the run," he says firmly, without blinking.

"Did you inform the police?"

"No. I don't trust the commissioner in charge of the case. Maybe someone else is involved, but don't worry. Give me a little more time. I'll find the culprit."

He hopes to have been persuasive and able to change the subject. He doesn't intend to mention Consuelo. During dinner, he manages to distract her with trivialities. At the end, she asks him to accompany her to her room for a drink of liqueur. She argues that it's still early and she's not sleepy. Adrián searches her eyes. She takes a cigarette out of her purse. The detective's brain has gone back on alert like the flatline that announces death on an oscilloscope screen. The one that suddenly curves upward and emits a barely audible beep, indicating a possibility of life, of hope. However, the way she casually and relaxedly blows the smoke to the side, without meeting his eyes, dispels his suspicions again.

Upon reaching the room, Sofía removes her shoes without sitting down, using her feet, while heading to the bar. Adrián watches the maneuver, focused on the sway of her firm glutes and the runway-like shoulder blades, bare due to the design of the open-back dress. She pours the liqueur. He opens the door to the terrace. He steps out and admires the panoramic view. He rests his elbows on the balcony. The night is just slightly cool. He lights a cigarette and contemplates the Montevideo Bay, the port cranes, and in the distance, the white fortress on the hill that gave the city its name. She arrives with two small glasses of Cointreau. They barely clink the glasses in a silent toast. Sofía also leans on the balcony, and they agree that the view is beautiful. They point out other iconic spots in the distance. Sofía takes a deep breath of the night air and lets out a long sigh. She asks for a puff of his cigarette. She wipes the lipstick off the filter and hands it back to him. They empty the glasses, and she goes back to refill them. Returning, she notices that he is staring at her, scanning her from head to toe, leaning against the balcony. She hands him the liqueur, but this time she maintains minimal distance between their bodies. Their eyes meet for several seconds. In the end, it's Adrián who gives in and looks away. He maneuvers around Sofía like a boxer escaping the ropes. He thanks her for inviting him, kisses her on the cheek, and says it's already late. He walks to the door. As he begins to open it, Sofía, standing behind him, firmly places her hand over the opening. Adrián turns his head. She takes control of the door and locks it. "Tonight, I'm not sleeping alone," she says resolutely, leaving no room for argument.

# XXXI

THEY EXPLORED THE MOST intimate corners as if they were strangers. At first, he barely nibbled, subtly, on her thigh. Then he kissed his way up to her groin with short pecks. She reciprocated. Minutes later, they were entangled, moaning, violent yet tender, as if they were wounded, consumed by intense pain. It was an overflowing crescendo, a climax that slowly faded until they were left breathless, succumbing to a calm embrace, overwhelmed by the cloying secretions of their bodies. Sofía turned over onto her stomach, rested her cheek on the pillow, filled her lungs with fresh air, and let it all out in a deflating, affectionate sigh.

"Oh, Adrián . . . the things you do to me!" she said, now relaxed, and half-closed her eyes. Gradually, she drifted off, lulled by his caresses, barely grazing her skin with the tips of his fingers.

At dawn, lying on his back in bed, with his hands behind his head, Adrián relived the images of the previous night. Sofía lay asleep, curled against his body. He wasn't superstitious, and he certainly hadn't dreamed it, but at times he tried to understand what had happened. No, it was real. He had spent the night with the only woman who had ever shaken his world, giving meaning to making future plans. Yet, at times, she didn't seem like the same Sofía. Is that the effect of time on two people who have loved each other? Intimacy cracks, and years later, it's almost like starting over.

Sofía began to open her eyelids as the rising sun seeped through the gaps in the curtains. She rubbed her eyes and kissed the detective's neck.

"Should I order breakfast to be brought up to the room?" she asked, meanwhile toying with her fingers, making curls in the hair on his chest. Adrián raised his eyebrows and widened his eyes, agreeing to the idea.

They had breakfast in bed, wrapped in elegant white robes with the Victoria Plaza logo stamped on the side of the lapel. He eyed the tray greedily, focused on its contents: scrambled eggs, Swiss cheese, prosciutto, and a warm croissant to spread with butter and fig jam, his favorite.

"You're still the same, Adrián. Sex always whets your appetite," she said, having already finished, watching him, propped up on her side on the pillow, her chin in her hand. Without looking at her, he nodded, chewing enthusiastically on a piece of cheese wrapped in prosciutto.

Later, she came out of the shower and began to dress. Adrián watched her intently, already dressed, sitting on a chair. Sofía felt his gaze and turned towards him.

"And Anthony?" the detective asked, serious, expressionless, studying her eyes.

She looked at him for a few seconds. Then, she approached and asked him to help zip up her dress. She then took out a cigarette, lit it, and opened the French door to the balcony. She remained silent for a few minutes, caught up in the incoherence of inhaling smoke while eagerly breathing in the healthy morning air. She looked at the detective again and gave a cynical smile.

"Anthony is ten thousand miles away, behaving just as badly as I am."

Adrián lowered his gaze. A feeling of guilt washed over him. The cause-and-effect relationship: his infidelity had led Sofía to end up in the hands of another jerk like him. She seemed to read his mind. She approached, took his chin, and caressed his cheek, meeting his eyes.

"No, it's not your fault. You can't keep judging yourself so harshly. You're not responsible for everything that happens in my life. We don't have that much control over things, Adrián."

He raised his eyebrows and shook his head, disbelieving the argument.

"Human carnal discipline hangs by a thread," Sofía continued, "at the mercy of the whims of the wind." She paused, lost in thought. "Wow! How poetic I've become," she said now with a sarcastic expression. "The wind, my ass! More like, our genitals."

He remained stunned, as if a strange, unknown voice was speaking with Sofía's body. She noticed his uncertainty. She caressed his face again and insisted that he had to learn to forgive himself. He jumped out of bed, disgusted, unable to figure out what bothered him more. The fact that he was responsible for Sofía's metamorphosis or that the cherished image he had of her in his memory was shattered. Can someone change so much in three years of separation?

He wasn't a puritan, but reflexively, he liked the idealistic, loyal, noble-hearted Sofía. On the other hand, what right did he have to expect or demand more from her?

"You weren't like this. I'm not judging you. If you ended up with another asshole like me, you have every right, but I can't swallow that I'm not responsible for your disillusionment. You believed in honor, in loyalty."

"Oh, Adrián," she said, almost impatiently. "If lawyers retained the honor, values, and virtues of our youth, we wouldn't get anywhere. We couldn't defend all that miserable human scum that bangs on our office doors. It was hard to accept, but now, nearing forty, I've realized that we're all more or less the same. At this point, what binds me to Anthony is a good relationship. He cheats on me, no doubt about it, but at least he's good to me. He protects me, in his own way. He treats me well. You and I are no longer for childish romances, Adrián. Our relationship was nice while it lasted, but it's a dead and buried fantasy."

After a while, Adrián left the Victoria Plaza, wondering if given Sofía's apparent personality change she would have been affected by learning the truth about her father. In any case, he wouldn't be the one to reveal the secret. He crossed Plaza Independencia towards the parking lot. If he had eyes on his back, he would have seen her watching him from the window with tear-filled eyes. The only recourse for the tough: to cry in private. The detective crossed the Ciudadela Gate, distant, obsessed with clinging to a hope that Sofía was pretending to be something she wasn't. But doubt returned as well. Had she become hard, relentless, true to the stereotype of the executive woman? Was the dormant Ferraro gene finally surfacing?

Upon arriving at the hotel, an old, overweight woman, dyed redhead, heavily made-up, and squeezed into a parrot-green dress threatening to burst at the seams, was waiting for him at the entrance.

"Are you Adrián Fontana?"

The detective nodded, and the woman handed him an envelope and quickly walked away. Adrián looked at the envelope on both sides. Both faces were blank. When he looked up, he reacted. He ordered her to stop, but it was too late. The old woman had already gotten into a car that was starting.

# XXXII

ADRIÁN BEGAN TO READ Consuelo's letter. It was written in a formal tone, occasionally sophisticated, which contrasted with her usual way of speaking. Like so many other villagers, Consuelo had a beautiful and elegant handwriting and a syntax and spelling precision that did not align in the least with her humble upbringing. The opposite of the presumption of Montevideo's patricians that good manners, education, or intellect must be inevitably tied only to them. The letter evidenced that, in the solitude of her tiny room in the Ferraro household, the maid had read and accumulated some culture.

"Mr. Adrián, I imagine you are looking for me like a bloodhound, sniffing out every corner of Montevideo. I know you haven't gone to the police. Otherwise, I would have found out by now. I know very well that you are already aware of the culprits of the crime. How could you not be when I was there in the basement, listening to everything. That stormy night still rings in my head. Alonso wasn't expecting me, but I had decided to go see him despite the storm. After descending to the basement, his shouts alerted me. I carefully turned the doorknob. It was unlocked. I opened the door just a few centimeters. Amidst drool, snot, and blood spatters, Néstor confessed to the crime. Everything was lost. I knew you would be relentless. Should I have entered and helped him? I still wonder if I should have approached from behind and hit you with something heavy, but I lack the cold blood to approach unnoticed. I doubt that would have changed things; it probably would have been useless. I couldn't move, as if my feet were stapled to the floor. That's when I heard those other footsteps. Heavy heels, I heard them almost rounding the curve of the pipes, and I was very afraid. I still remember how my legs trembled, hiding behind that column. Stern and another man as huge as him were almost at Alonso's apartment door. I held my breath, pressed myself against the concrete pillar. My heartbeat was so loud it felt like it might give me away. The tiptoe retreat to the stairs was an eternity. I fled desperately through the hall. Mr. Adrián, I knew they were following me; I could smell them. Already on the street, I ran and ran and ran under the torrential rain. I, who despite being thin, always came last in my childhood races back in Rivera. What irony! Now I remember Rivera. My Rivera, that dull and grey place I joyfully escaped from, which now presents itself as a lost paradise. What would my parents say, Mr. Adrián, if they saw me now, an accomplice to two murders? And my siblings? Would they have protected me? I know I am alone. The years, the distance, and the bad memories of a childhood full of beatings have annihilated even fraternal bonds. I don't even know where they live anymore. But back to my desperate escape along the promenade. I didn't care about the brutal force of the waves crashing against the shore. I wasn't even scared of the thunder I had feared since I was a child. I swear I could hear Stern's steps and the other's breath close behind me. Reaching Gomensoro Square, I was drenched, with my hair flat on my forehead. I couldn't run anymore. I had no strength left. When I turned around, resigned to my fate, the street was empty. No one was following me. I then climbed uphill through Pocitos, from the promenade to Artigas Boulevard. My clothes clung to my body, but I decided not to return to my apartment. I had my documents, some money, and a credit card with me. Now I could use that piece of plastic without fear of the limit. The debts, the creditors had just become secondary. I only leave this filthy hovel at night, to buy food that I then vomit in the early morning. I return to bed, weak, exhausted. Yet my brain remains awake, cornering me with memories. Some things pierce me like a hammer continuously driving an endless nail. Alonso's pleas, Carlota's strangled face. Then Lucrecia. Two murders. Why did the order of things suddenly go off course without warning? Had I done something to deserve all of God's wrath? Reacting to a secret that had to remain inviolate wasn't justified in the Lord's eyes? A sin of another that ultimately exploded in my face. To me, Mr. Adrián! To me, who had kept it hidden deep within since that day I heard Carlota trying to bribe old Ferraro. Everything became clear to me when I heard that argument, hidden behind a curtain. The old man and his daughter thought they were alone in the house, and I heard Carlota demanding a BMW, otherwise she would make public the incest. Don Ferraro cursed her without denying it. It was on that crucial day when I finally understood in an instant, in a clear and clarifying flash, the answer to the question everyone was asking. Why so many material differences between the two sisters? I didn't know if the incest had been rape or consensual, or who had initiated it, but I, the Ferraros' maid, now saw two things clearly: Carlota would always have old Ferraro by the balls, and more importantly: I would do everything possible to protect my child Javier from that terrible secret. Yes, because he was my child, damn it! I bathed him, dressed him for school, parted his hair admiring its silkiness. I took him to birthday parties, told him bedtime stories, placed cold compresses on his forehead when he was sick. He was mine by right! The gestation in another womb, a biological misfortune! A foreign event. But I, Consuelo Flores, deserved the diploma of motherhood. Certified by Christ, Our Lord! I repeated this to myself over and over as I spent my life, my youth, in the shadow of the Ferraro's. But I swear I never premeditated Carlota's murder. However, although it may seem unbelievable, Mr. Adrián, I remember that seeing her lifeless body didn't affect me, despite that horrible final grimace: it was about Javier's happiness. Still, I tried to convince Alonso not to kill the one-arm woman. Or did I imagine it? I think I tried. 'We are not murderers,' I insisted to him. I repeated it to myself day and night. Anyway, it doesn't matter anymore. We have crossed the border of good to a point of no return. Here I am, flailing, unable to swim, in a sea dyed with blood that freezes my bones. There is no turning back. I was not the executioner's hand, but I do not absolve myself of guilt. I know I will burn in hell. I have as much blood on my hands as a certain Lady Macbeth I once saw at the Solís theater. I was still young and dreamed of being cultured like Sofía or Carlota, to speak like them. I secretly tried on their clothes. I hoped that one day I would escape the destiny that my cradle had condemned me to, to mediocrity, to the loneliness of my existence. I was only happy when Javier was born. His childhood was the best time of my life. At night I lie on this sagging, lice-infested cot that serves as a bed. I relive Javier's disdain, his selfishness, his cruelty towards me and the rest of the servants. I feel my expression harden for a moment, as if I hated him. Then I lie still, with the bathroom light on, staring at the damp stain on the ceiling. I create human shapes from the moss. Sometimes I seem to see a large pool of coagulated blood. Other times, I see eyes watching me from the blackened ceiling. Could it be God watching, or the Holy Spirit I was told about as a child? Does He come to pity me or to jump on me with His divine justice? Thou shalt not kill! I have violated that commandment! But no, I was not the executioner's hand. Does that matter to God? Sometimes I dream of sleeping, but then I get tangled up, drowning in the morbid web that ensnares my spirit. Do not worry, Mr. Adrián. Sofía will never know about the incest. She will not hear it from me, and I hope, I implore, that she won't hear it from you either. I know you care about the girl Sofía. The only one in the family who skipped the twisted Ferraro gene. With whom I laughed, with whom I confided on more than one occasion, grateful each time she rescued me from Doña Renata's abusive claws. I have asked my neighbor Maruja to hand you this letter personally. Please, destroy it after reading it! I hope Sofía finds happiness. I do not expect her to forgive me. All the best to you too. As for me, I have reached the end of my weary bones. Tired of my sleepless nights, I shake this tragedy from my mind. Standing on the stool, I will be two in one: executioner and condemned. For the first time in my life, I am the owner of my destiny."

The detective remained tense as he read the last sentence. It was obvious what it meant. An inevitable end. Consuelo had the last word before leaving the world of the living, wherever she might be. He took a deep breath. A sense of relief washed over his body. This sudden well-being brought a feeling of guilt, but he consoled himself, thinking that everything was now irreparable. Besides, Consuelo no longer suffered, he reassured himself. He let his arms fall to the sides of the armchair. He stretched his legs and rested them on the coffee table. The burden accumulated over the past few days finally drained from his body. He looked at the envelope. It had no sender. He took the lighter from his pants pocket, lit it, and held it to the bottom edge of the paper. He held it in his hand as it burned. When the flame almost reached his fingers, he let it drop to the floor. He gathered the ashes, threw them into the toilet, and pressed the flush button. He remained pensive, watching the swirl of water swallow Consuelo's confession. It was only in that moment of introspection that he fully realized the miserable life the maid had endured.

"May you find peace on the other side, skinny," he murmured as he lowered the toilet lid.

It was already two in the afternoon, but he had no appetite. The copious breakfast at the Victoria Plaza still lingered in his stomach. He decided to go for a walk along the promenade. The sky had shaken off the clouds, and the sun spread its warm mantle over Pocitos. He delighted in the gentle April breeze refreshing his face while he meditated on his final strategy. The time had come to report the doorman to the police to lend credibility to his version. He needed to close the case in Sofía's eyes and leave Consuelo out of the plot. Alonso was the sole murderer. He would explain to Commissioner Bermúdez that he had sneaked into Alonso's room and discovered the possible murder weapon: a fishing line leader. Alonso's absence increased his status as a suspect. Before calling the commissioner, he would alert Stern. He counted on his agreement. It was obvious to him that the mobster would have made sure not to leave traces of his revenge. Besides, Stern was the godfather of the commissioner's daughter. Bermúdez would never incriminate him. He smiled, satisfied. Everything fit.

He walked to the little port of Buceo and leisurely returned to the hotel. His stay in Montevideo was coming to an end. He tried to absorb what surrounded him: the cawing of seagulls, the salt in the air, the waves, the fishermen returning to shore in their small boats. Everything he wouldn't see in Richmond. It was hard to accept that little by little, the little country was peeling away from him. A Montevideo without Sofía, without his mother. What was the point?

Back at the hotel, he took a long nap. For the first time in many days, he slept deeply.

By nightfall, he was visiting Rabbit Vergara's apartment and told him about Consuelo's letter. His friend patted him on the back. Rabbit went to the sideboard and returned with a bottle in hand.

"Even if it's sad, it's for the best for everyone, brother," said Rabbit. He jubilantly waved the bottle like a championship trophy. "Johnny Walker, blue label. This is like syrup for the stomach, Fontana!"

Adrián didn't hesitate and began to pour the drinks. Rabbit went to the kitchen. After a few minutes, he returned with an appetizer of dates skewered with pieces of Roquefort cheese and a wooden board with slices of sausage. The detective was already on his second glass.

"Are you drinking with a straw?" said Rabbit. "Don't despair, my friend. I have another one stored in the sideboard. My smuggler friend gets them for me."

"Dates with Roquefort. You've become quite sophisticated, Vergara," said Adrián, savoring the combination.

"One does what one can."

The detective refilled his glass. They were sitting on the balcony overlooking the Pocitos beach promenade. He took a generous sip and gazed at the silver line of the horizon. A huge full moon spread its trail over the calm waters of the Rio de la Plata.

After a while, Mr. Walker was almost at the bottom of the bottle, and Rabbit dared to ask if there was any chance of reconciliation with Sofía. He knew his friend was private about his personal life and that such questions usually infuriated him, except when he had ingested substantial doses of alcohol. Then, sometimes, on rare occasions, he took the initiative and opened up a bit about his intimacy.

"I'm asking because when I picked her up at the airport, we chatted for a while, and it seemed to me that her relationship with that Anthony guy wasn't wonderful," said Rabbit. "You know she has always felt very comfortable confiding in me. Do you remember when we used to go dancing together at Lancelot? Before I broke up with Sandra. Those were the days, brother! We felt like we ruled the world."

Adrián smiled with his head down.

"I don't know," Rabbit continued. "I asked her about her husband, and I got the impression that she's not happy with the gringo. You know my intuition never fails."

"There's no possible fix, Vergara," said Adrián, his gaze clouded. He remained distant, silent for a few seconds, mentally absorbed by a black hole in his memory. Then he returned to the present and gave a cynical smile. "I screwed up with her best friend from university."

He drank the rest of his glass. He stretched his legs and rested them on the balcony railing. He raised his arms and put his hands behind his head, once again abstracted, eyes on the sea. He fell silent again.

"Come on, go on!" demanded Rabbit, drumming his fingers impatiently on the coffee table. "What do you mean you screwed her friend?"

"They studied together in our apartment in Richmond. The girl kept coming after me until one day she found me."

Rabbit's facial muscles contracted in a chain reaction. He frowned, squinted his eyes, wrinkled his nose, clenched his teeth, and drew a devilish smile.

"Checkmate! If you seek, you shall find," he said, raising his fist.

Adrián closed his eyes and shook his head.

"We're a bad species, Vergara," he continued after a pause. "We see a nice ass and throw everything overboard like idiots. For a five-minute fuck with a girl, we have nothing in common with."

Rabbit looked puzzled.

"But that's how men are, Adrián. That's how God made us," he said, stretching to skewer a piece of sausage with a toothpick. "There's nothing better than screwing. Man is like a dog, buddy. Variety is the spice of life. Are you gay now?"

He vigorously patted the detective on the back and let out another laugh.

"No, idiot. That's not it," said Adrián as he poured another generous measure of blue label into both glasses. "If God created man, as you say, then sex was invented by the devil."

"Without sex, the species would go extinct, Adrián. How else would we reproduce?"

"I don't know. Ask your creator. If he was able to create his son without Joseph the carpenter's intervention, he surely has the recipe. He could have done the same with the rest of us mortals."

Rabbit looked at him, stupefied.

"Oh no! You're crazier than a goat, brother," he said, widening his eyes.

The detective found his friend's reaction amusing and laughed heartily.

"Maybe, Vergara. Don't take me too seriously. Anyway, you know that if you put a hot woman in front of me, I'll forget all this cheap philosophy and nail her, so she doesn't fly away. That doesn't change the fact that the male of our species is a piece of crap," he said, drawing a mocking smile as he threw a bread crumb he had been kneading in his fingers. Rabbit dodged it and threw a coaster at him. They both laughed with the same mischievous look they had when they teased each other in high school, throwing pieces of paper or erasers behind the teacher's back.

"Women aren't all sweet and innocent, Adrián. They know how to cheat too. Don't fool yourself," insisted Rabbit.

"I'm not saying they don't, Vergara, but generally, women give themselves more for love. They also have a different discipline for sex. They're not the same. We see a swaying ass and draw our .38 caliber without thinking twice about where to put it."

"Let's see . . . a .38 if we're talking about me," interrupted Rabbit with a jocular laugh. "In your case, a mere .22 caliber."

Adrián threw the bottle cap at him. Rabbit dodged it and once again flashed his healthy incisors, reveling in his way of teasing.

"And what did Sofía do when she found out? Did she catch you in the act?"

"Yep. With the other girl riding on top of me."

"And what did she say?"

"Nothing. She said nothing, neither at that moment nor ever again."

After fumbling a bit inside his jacket, the detective pulled out a cigar. Despite Adrián's reputation for handling large amounts of alcohol, Rabbit noticed his friend's body beginning to falter. He took his lighter from his jacket and lit it for him. Adrián exhaled a long puff of smoke and looked at him intently.

"Have you ever closely observed the expression on a woman's face when she finds out you cheated on her? It's the saddest, most desperate thing in the world, brother. Their eyes say more than a thousand words. The betrayal, the helplessness. The fragility reflected in their pupils."

They looked at each other intently. Rabbit understood it was not the moment for another joke. He diverted his gaze. Now he was the one who took the cigar sticking out of his shirt pocket. He lit it, took a few quick puffs, and then looked back at his friend.

"I suppose by now she must have gotten over it. Women are strong, Adrián."

The detective redirected his gaze beyond the balcony but remained focused on the line of thought that, even after three years of separation, still tormented him.

"She gave up everything for me. Social status, financial security. When her parents opposed our relationship, she stood up to them like a lioness. She didn't think about her well-being, or her inheritance, or anything. She was a woman of honor. Still is, even though she tries to sell me otherwise! A genetic leap, a chromosomal exception to the rest of the family. She was exposed to the same bad upbringing as Carlota. Raised to feel superior to others. Yet none of it stuck to her. You have no idea how the workers adored her! And all for what? To end up betrayed by this son of a bitch who's drinking your whiskey."

"Hey, take it easy, brother. Don't be so hard on yourself! Nobody's perfect."

"You know what's the worst part?" Adrián continued, not listening to what Rabbit's mouth was emitting. "If she forgave me tomorrow and we got back together, at the first opportunity another beautiful ass came in front of me, I'd screw up again. No, my friend! Things are better this way. I already broke her heart once. Once is enough and too much."

"Okay, man! You're more dramatic than a tango!" Rabbit said, trying to lighten the atmosphere. He began to hum "Cambalache": "The world was and will be a mess, I already know . . . "

Adrián joined in the chorus: " . . . in the year five hundred ten and in two thousand too. That there have always been thieves, traitors and swindlers, happy and bitter, values and double-dealing . . . "

They paused, refilled their lungs with air, patted each other on the back, raised their glasses, and attacked the next line with vigor: "But that the 20th century is a display of insolent evil, nobody can deny it. We live tangled in a meringue and in the same mud, all mixed up!"

Then, both released a tremendous and comradely laugh, harsh and raspy, delighted by the drunkenness. They clinked their glasses again with vigor.

From the balcony above, a man's irritated voice was heard.

"Hey, stop the racket and go sleep it off, for fuck's sake! Some people must work tomorrow, damn it!"

"Well, if you have to work, tough luck, you idiot, slave!" Rabbit retorted. He playfully embraced the detective and guided him inside while closing the sliding terrace door with his other hand.

# XXXIII

THE SCANDALOUS EXPLOSIONS FROM the exhaust pipe of an old junker managed to wake Adrián from a deep sleep. He blinked and looked towards the window. It was already daylight. He felt his head loose. The last traces of alcohol were still lingering in his body. He checked the time and cursed when he saw it was eleven. He had agreed to have lunch with Sofía. He sat on the bed for a moment, scratching his head. He remembered the previous evening at Rabbit's apartment. In Richmond, he had a few American friends he could consider close, but "Rabbit" Vergara was a chapter apart. They had grown up together since puberty, and he was the closest thing to a brother he had.

He walked clumsily to the bathroom mirror and studied his face. He shook his head and widened his eyes to shake off the drowsiness. He tidied up his mustache, which was disheveled against the grain from the pressure on the pillow. His body ached as if he'd been run over by a bull, but it had been worth it. A blue label wasn't an everyday thing.

He was surprised to hear himself whistling in the shower. He couldn't remember the last time he had done that. Was he happy because Sofía no longer judged him as harshly as she had three years ago, or was it something else? He refused to analyze it. He was whistling, and realizing it pleased him.

Upon arriving at the Victoria Plaza, he announced himself at reception. Sofía had said to come up. He took the elevator to the ninth floor and looked for room 909 upon exiting. The door was ajar. He knocked twice and peeked into the room. She was smoking, leaning on the table with her head resting on her hand.

"Come in, sit down," she said in a distant tone. "Did you read the newspaper?"

Adrián noticed the copy of El País on the table.

"No, not yet. I was out with Rabbit last night and slept in."

He couldn't read the headlines backward, but he knew what they were about.

He sat in front of her, studying her eyes as he picked up the newspaper.

"They found Consuelo hanged in her room," Sofía said with a mixture of calm and resignation.

Adrián grabbed the paper and read the headline. Then he hurriedly flipped through the pages, looking for the crime section. He read the first paragraphs describing the discovery of the body.

Consuelo had left a note confessing her complicity in Carlota Ferraro's murder. She pointed to Alonso as the executioner and explained they had killed her because she owed them several months of wages and had caught them trying to steal her jewelry. The note ended by saying she couldn't live with her conscience any longer and signed it at the bottom. Adrián lingered for a few seconds on the servant's signature. Her harmonious handwriting reminded him of his mother's, who, like Consuelo, had not finished primary school. He closed the paper and sighed. Consuelo had fabricated a very believable lie.

She had been found in a miserable room at the back of a clandestine brothel on Piedras Street, two blocks from the port. There, they offered services from prostitutes without health cards to clients from the Korean fishing boats anchored in the bay.

That afternoon on the TV channels, Maruja Silveira, the madam of the brothel, was interviewed by the press. Adrián recognized her. The same old redhead, disheveled, with few teeth in her mouth, who had given him the envelope. Before interviewing her, the newscast had introduced her past. As a young woman, she had also been on the front pages for killing a pimp who mistreated her.

"Sometimes I would take her a hot plate," the woman declared, besieged by microphones almost covering her face. "When she heard a police siren, she got very nervous. She always kept the curtains drawn. The poor girl suffered from insomnia. She was almost skeletal, with skin sticking to her bones. Sometimes I'd go to drink *mate* and keep her company for a while. Last night, she came to ask if I could take a message for her. She offered me money for the taxi. I refused, but she insisted. It was the last time I saw her. This morning, my colleagues found her hanging from a beam in the ceiling. She looked like she was sleeping, the poor thing."

When a journalist asked who the message was for, Maruja got angry. She replied that the deceased had asked for confidentiality, and she wasn't going to break her word.

"I may be a woman of the night, but my word is sacred, so take that question and shove it where the sun doesn't shine," she said, pointing her finger. She pushed the microphones away and made her way through the crowd.

"You were right to suspect the doorman. He was the killer," said Sofía. "I never would have imagined Consuelo capable of this. How sad, how that poor wretch ended!"

The detective was relieved that Sofía pitied the accomplice in her sister's murder. Not seeing her too affected. After all, Sofía had always predicted Carlota would end badly. He, on the other hand, still felt a certain remorseful peace coursing through his body.

The next morning, Adrián and Rabbit took Sofía to the airport. Before boarding, she took an envelope out of her purse.

"Inside are your fees as we discussed."

Adrián took the envelope and looked at it, distracted.

Then he looked up and returned it. After all, he hadn't been able to catch the culprit, he explained.

"Come on, Adrián. A deal is a deal. You thought the killer was Alonso, and you were right. Your responsibility ends here. The police will catch him."

The two friends exchanged a fleeting look of complicity.

"You've already taken care of my expenses in Montevideo," said Adrián. "That's enough. Traveling to Uruguay wasn't a burden. You know I always like to return home."

Rabbit followed the conversation with wide eyes and an O-shaped mouth. His gaze alternated between what one and the other said as if watching a tennis match from the sideline.

"Well, let's see . . ." interrupted Rabbit. "If Mr. Nincompoop doesn't accept the payment from the distinguished lady, then his humble assistant here will gladly accept it. After all, I've been a key piece in the investigation," he added seriously. He raised his eyebrows arrogantly and extended his hand towards the envelope.

Sofía knew Rabbit's skill for serious joking without a muscle twitching. Adrián, however, seemed to fall into the trap and slapped his friend's hand away.

"Put that paw in your pocket, idiot."

Rabbit burst into laughter.

"Relax, tin kettle. It was just a joke," said Rabbit, choking on his laughter.

Sofía played along.

"Come on, Adrián, you don't think Rúben was trying to take advantage, do you? He's as innocent as a baby."

"Yeah, yeah, lots of jokes . . . but don't trust this herbivorous rodent. He's faster than Speedy Gonzales," said Adrián.

"Pronto Gómez!" corrected Rabbit. "Dick Tracy's loyal sidekick was called Pronto Gómez." He gestured as if talking into a radio communicator on his wrist, just like the famous comic strip character, and added, "Dick Tracy calling Pronto Gómez, calling Pronto Gómez!"

The airport speakers announced boarding for the flight to the United States. Sofía approached Adrián and kissed him on the cheek. She held his eyes for a few seconds.

"Before you leave, go where you know you need to go . . ."

Adrián said nothing. Sofía turned to Rabbit.

"And you, give me a big hug and promise you'll take care of your friend in his last hours in Montevideo," she said, extending her arms to Rabbit's unreachable height.

Rúben Vergara bent down, and she hugged him long and effusively. When she let go, Rabbit turned to Adrián and flashed his exuberant keyboard smile.

"See? She likes me better than you. A simple kiss on the cheek for Fontana. A long, affectionate hug for me."

Sofía laughed and pushed him back, amused by the big guy's joke. She grabbed her suitcase off the floor and headed to security. Before disappearing through the door, she turned back.

"Rúben, check your coat pocket," she said with a mischievous smile and disappeared behind the customs screen.

Rabbit put his hand in his pocket. When he pulled it out, he was holding the envelope Adrián had refused.

"Damn you, Vergara! That's why the hug lasted so long. She was slipping the envelope into your pocket, you idiot!"

Rabbit threw his arms in the air in resignation. Then he handed him the envelope.

"Take it, fool, and stop being so poetic. Do the bills in Richmond pay themselves?"

They walked towards the exit. Adrián was still grumbling.

"Damn you, Rabbit."

They headed down Avenida de las Américas until they reached the fork where you could return to Pocitos via Avenida Italia or along the coast road.

"Take the coast road," said Adrián.

"The coast road is much longer," protested Rabbit.

"Take the coast road, damn it. Who knows how long it will be before I see the Montevideo coast again."

"As you wish, Mr. Tracy. Here Pronto Gómez is at your service," said Rabbit, drumming his fingers on the wheel.

During the drive along the coast road, Adrián remained silent with a furrowed brow. Rabbit, who occasionally glanced at him, deduced it was due to Sofía's departure.

Upon arriving at the hotel before saying goodbye, Adrián asked if he knew any place that edited video tapes.

"There's one near the hotel that has machines to convert VHS to DVD and lets you cut scenes. They also rent the equipment if you want to do it at home. That's what my sister did to edit her wedding recording."

"I like the second option, Vergara. Do me a favor and rent it for twenty-four hours. I'll give you the money afterward. Tomorrow, you and I will cut a tape at your apartment."

Rabbit nodded without prying. He had a good idea of which video Adrián meant. He knew his friend well enough not to bombard him with questions when his body language radiated bad temper. He knew that the next day he would understand what Adrián had in mind.

# XXXIV

"WHEN I GROW UP, I'm going to be a detective," he had told his father as they left the cinema after watching *The Maltese Falcon*. His father took him everywhere: to see classic Hollywood noir films, to the exclusive men's clubs perched on the rocks of Ramírez Beach, or fishing at the breakwater at the end of Sarandí Street.

"Should we invite Mom?" the boy sometimes asked.

"This is men's stuff, Adrián. You and I are buddies, aren't we?" his father would reply, ruffling his son's hair. The boy enjoyed his childhood with his neighborhood friends, but nothing compared to outings with his father. They were his favorite pastime. Despite being a construction worker who hadn't gone beyond fifth grade, his father had the wisdom to talk to his son as an equal.

Adrián also enjoyed watching him in the kitchen. As a good descendant of Neapolitans, his father loved making pizza. The construction worker would clear the rustic pine table where they ate lunch, spread flour over nearly the entire surface to prevent the dough from sticking, and start mixing the ingredients. Adrián would rest his elbows on the edge, hold his face in his hands, and watch as his father's robust fingers stretched the dough from the center outwards and then skillfully smoothed it with a rolling pin. Before putting it in the oven, he would boast about his creation. He'd raise his right arm and spin the round dough mass on his index finger, a difficult maneuver he had learned from a pizza master in the neighborhood pizzeria. He had worked there in his teens to help his parents before dedicating himself to construction.

Other times, he taught his son how to slide pieces of dough over the tines of a fork to shape gnocchi and use the metal wheel to cut and grid ravioli. The construction worker's culinary skills were so adept that his wife always said, "I learned to cook from my husband."

Adrián grew up in a fantasy-induced haze. It was that time in life when parents are still our heroes, before the illusion shatters against the infallible maturity.

When he turned thirteen, their adventures became more sporadic. They hardly went to the movies to see Humphrey Bogart anymore, and his father started coming home only at midnight. Adrián wouldn't fall asleep until he heard the key turn in the door. One night, his father didn't come back. Not the next day either. A week later, mother and son found out he had gone to Australia with a waitress from the port market.

A decade later, the construction worker returned to Montevideo to die in his homeland, alone and sick with lung cancer. He sent a message to his son, saying he would wait for him at La Mesita, which is what Adrián called a black, flat plateau among the rocks of Ramírez Beach. It was there his father had taught him to dive. The young man didn't go to the meeting. Nor did he attend the wake or the burial at Buceo Cemetery. By then, Adrián and Sofía were already dating. Since that day, he never set foot in a cemetery again, neither in Uruguay nor abroad.

Now, seventeen years later, the detective walks briskly through the inner streets of the necropolis, following the instructions given to him at the entrance. In his right hand, he carries a plastic tube, the kind architects use to transport plans or rolled drawings. Rubén Vergara follows at a distance behind the wheel, driving in first gear. The detective nostalgically contemplates the statues and sculptures that had captivated him so much the first time he visited the place, with his third-grade study group: replicas of *The Pietà* sculpted by Eduardo Yepes, the enigmatic tomb of Francisco Piria, and the allegory of the Desperate Man. Further ahead, he passes the enormous black marble pantheon, crowned by a sphinx and Egyptian motifs on all four sides. He recalls the history teacher's comment, a Galician naturalized Uruguayan: "Damn! This cemetery is just like the ones in Galicia and the rest of the motherland. Take note, lads! Here lies the old world. Emigrants even bring their cemeteries in their suitcases." Adrián confirmed this years later when he visited the Iberian Peninsula and the Italian boot. The culture of the Mediterranean peoples had been transplanted to the land of the Charrúas.

It's mid-morning, and the sun is still playing hide and seek with the clouds, but little by little, the sea breeze returns the blue to the sky.

Rabbit notices his friend stops upon reaching the end of the path, right in front of the cemetery's southern wall, which marks the boundary between the dead and the sea, between unchanging peace and the waters' perpetual motion. Below, on the rambla, the famous Curve of Death can be seen.

Adrián removes a handful of dry leaves with his hand, uncovering the first two letters of his father's surname. He sits on the step of the adjacent tomb and takes out a cigarette. A few meters away, sitting on a luxurious pantheon, a tabby cat skins a sparrow, undisturbed by the detective's presence.

"How are you, old man," he says, barely audible, scratching the back of his neck. "Prime location. You always liked being near the coast."

He doesn't bite his lip as he usually does when trying to hold back tears. He's calm. He smiles serenely, one of those smiles that appear after having seen and traveled a long stretch of the road. Then, he takes a pack of La Paz Suave cigarettes, his father's favorite black tobacco, from his jacket pocket. He opens the box, takes out a cigarette, lights it with his own, and places it on the edge of the marble, with the ember outwards so it won't extinguish.

"Here's a black one, old man," he laughs and adds, "I'll join you with a blond. As you used to say: 'Blacks are only for those with balls.'"

He slides off the step onto the grass and lies there for a while, looking at the sky, his legs stretched out, barely touching his father's tomb. After a while, he sits up and rests his arms on the grass behind him. Rabbit remains at the wheel. Sometimes Adrián shakes his head and shrugs, as if trying to explain something. After a few minutes, the detective stands up. He uncaps the plastic tube and takes out a waterproof poster he bought at the Tristan Narvaja market. He unrolls it and places it on the tombstone. He steps back a few paces and returns with four stones, placing them on the four edges of the poster to secure it against the sea winds. He looks once more and smiles at Humphrey Bogart and Ingrid Bergman, embraced tête-à-tête in *Casablanca*. At the bottom of the poster, the detective has written: "Old man, after all I've seen in my forty years, the Nazarene is right; let him who is without sin cast the first stone."

Then, he turns around and heads for Rabbit's car. He gets into the vehicle, and his friend looks at him with tenderness.

"Come on, start the car, Pronto Gomez! And wipe that sentimental look off your face," says Adrián, patting him on the shoulder and insisting, "Come on, so we get to the airport early and have a whiskey before I leave."

"At your command, Dick Tracy," Rabbit says, giving a military salute. He eagerly turns the wheel and heads for the exit.

# XXXV

When the phone rang, he was trimming his mustache in front of the bathroom cabinet mirror. He picked up and immediately recognized the nasal voice of "Cheeks" Stern on the other end of the line. The call surprised him. He wondered how Stern had gotten his phone number.

"Good morning, detective. How's everything in Gringoland?"

"Damn, what a surprise. Everything's fine here, Stern. To what do I owe the honor? I'm charming, but I wouldn't have imagined that after two months you'd already miss me back home."

Cheeks burst out laughing, which turned into a phlegmy cough that mixed with his laughter and at times choked him.

"I need to quit smoking," he commented.

"And stop fornicating! You're getting old, and your heart's going to fail you," said Adrián. He put the phone on speaker and continued tidying his mustache.

"Never, Mike Hammer. At my age, I'm not about to turn into a Buddhist monk," Stern replied, still battling his phlegm. "You're going to receive a big package, sent by special mail to your apartment. It'll require your signature. Don't ignore the doorbell because you got plastered the night before."

"I promise to only drink milk until it arrives."

Cheeks let out another laugh, triggering another coughing fit. When he recovered, he said:

"Are you kidding me? Is it April Fool's Day in the United States?"

"No, seriously, Stern. Just milk and healing syrups. My stomach still hurts from the punches King Kong gave me. I can't handle alcohol."

Cheeks laughed skeptically and cleared more phlegm. Then Adrián inquired:

"A package for me? What's that about? My birthday is still a long way off."

"Relax, it's not for you, idiot. It's for you to take to your ex-girlfriend. That's where it belongs," Cheeks explained, having recovered from his coughing fit.

"The painting of the white wolf?" Immediately, a second question arose. "But how did you manage to get it out through Montevideo customs? They're very strict with permits for exporting artworks."

As soon as he finished the sentence, he realized it was a stupid question. Stern had bribable snitches everywhere.

"Get some coffee, man! You're kind of slow this morning," Cheeks retorted mockingly.

"Damn, your English is pretty good."

"I remember a bit from when old Stern sent me to the United States to lay low for a while. The question is offensive, brother. Cheeks's reach is long," the thug clarified with a chuckle.

"Touché. Major mistake on my part," said Adrián. "But why so much generosity? Are you getting soft in your old age?"

"Soft, my ass! Nobody should get any ideas, but I certainly appreciate loyalty. You kept your mouth shut, and both Bermúdez and I are grateful, capisce?" He paused, cleared his chest, and continued, "Regarding the painting, I've never been interested in art. I'm not as sophisticated as my friend the detective. Besides, it's only fair that her sister inherits it. That's what Carlota wanted. Agreed?"

"Agreed, Stern. And has there been any news about Javier's disappearance?"

"They saw him with his surfboard on the beaches of northern Brazil. He washed up on shore with a bullet hole in his forehead."

"And Bonilla?"

"Don't they sell newspapers there?"

"If you lived here, you should know. The Americans don't give a damn about what happens in their backyard. They only report on their own bubble."

"Yeah, that's true. I'd forgotten. Well, to catch you up on Bonilla: a woman named Juana handed a video to the police that incriminated him. The servants say that when he found out, he was yelling all over the house: 'He must have edited it, the bastard edited it!' When the police arrived at his residence to arrest him, he locked himself in his office and shot himself. Many of his Operation Condor buddies have also been convicted and are now rotting in Domingo Arenas prison," Stern said. He cleared his throat again and added, "Well, my friend, we'll leave it here. The call is long-distance, and it's going to cost me a fortune."

"Yes, watch your budget. After all, you're a proletarian. You're not swimming in money."

"Take care, detective. Don't get lost."

"See you one of these days, Stern. My regards to King Kong. Tell him I'll bring a bag of candy when I travel back home."

He hung up and remained pensive. Once again, he marveled at the unpredictability of human nature. In a corner of his violent and ruthless soul, the mobster had a sentimental streak.

# XXXVI

Sofía Ferraro lived in the elegant and historic Fan district, the most representative Victorian architecture neighborhood in Richmond. She was watering the plants in the greenhouse at the back when she heard the doorbell ring. She turned off the tap and went to answer the door. When she opened it, there was no one there. She saw the package resting on the accumulated pine needles on the porch. It was addressed to her, but she noticed it had no sender. She dragged it inside and left the door ajar. She carefully cut the meticulous packaging that had "Fragile" labels on all four sides.

Her eyes widened when she saw the painting.

"Oh my God!" she said, bringing her hand to her mouth. She peered out the door again and looked both ways down the street to discern who might have brought the package. Not a soul was in sight. Then, she lowered her head and stood in thought for a few seconds, stretching her lower lip with her thumb and index finger. She looked at the empty sidewalk again, smiled, and murmured, "Adrián, you cunning son of a bitch!"

The detective watched her, hidden behind some bushes on the opposite sidewalk. After Sofía went inside, he left his hiding place and walked away slowly with a mischievous smirk.

The intense June sun filtered with difficulty through the crowded foliage of the oaks, barely flirting with the sidewalks of Park Avenue. A fresh breeze helped dry the humidity of the previous days. The detective got into the Ford Mustang parked half a block from Sofía's house. When he reached Shockoe Bottom, he opened the car trunk and took out a can of paint, a brush, a roller, and a blue smock. He went up to his office and, before entering, made sure the sign with his name and profession hung straight on the door. While the coffee was heating, he picked up the Budweiser cans scattered on the floor. He also sorted and piled up all the creditors' bills strewn across his desk. Then he put on the blue smock and scanned the peeling walls.

"It's time," he murmured. He opened the can, barely dipped the tip of the brush, and tested the color in a corner. He nodded in approval. He rolled up the windowpanes. He put on a vinyl record of his favorite band: Creedence Clearwater Revival. He started painting, pausing now and then to sip coffee. The telephone's ring stood out in the quiet of Richmond's commercial district, deserted of office workers on weekends. Graciela's sensual voice came from the other end of the line.

"How's my favorite detective doing?"

Adrián found the comment amusing.

"How many detectives do you know?"

"Let's see . . . Pepe Carvalho, Sherlock Holmes, Philip Marlowe, Hercule Poirot, and some others I'm forgetting," Graciela said with her usual sharpness.

"What's new, girl?"

"I'll tell you that Manuel has given me three weeks of vacation, and I thought about visiting you. Can I?"

"You can. But we'll have to share the same bed. I don't have a guest room."

"That's okay, I'm petite. I don't take up much space. So, can I book the tickets?"

"Go ahead."

"Oh, what joy! My first trip to the United States," Graciela said. "Should I bring you something from Uruguay?"

"A jar of dulce de leche."

"I didn't know you had a sweet tooth."

"Dulce de leche has many uses. I'll show you later."

"Oh, I'm dying of curiosity. Well, I'm off to buy the tickets. I'll hang up now because Manuel is coming, and he scolds me if I make personal calls. Kisses and hugs."

"Bye, girl, behave yourself," said the detective. He hung up the receiver and turned up the volume on the record player. He returned to the ladder and dipped the brush into the can to continue with the edges of a corner.

John Fogerty's voice slipped through the window and caught the southern breeze. His raspy baritone voice could be heard from the high pillars of the railway bridge that overlooked Adrián's office. The melody also reached the unloading dock of an old tobacco warehouse on the banks of the James River. An old hippie was fishing for catfish standing on the edge. Hearing "The Midnight Special," the sixty-something started to sway his hips, caught up in the Rock and Roll rhythm.

# ABOUT THE AUTHOR

CARLOS GARABELLI WAS BORN in Montevideo, Uruguay. He grew up in the sixties and seventies, decades that the author considers significant in the socio-cultural transformations of the twentieth century, and in the formation of his personality. It was in this cosmopolitan Montevideo, populated by the children and grandchildren of immigrants, that from an early age, he looked beyond borders to rediscover and understand a national identity forged in the old world. A fervent believer in the concept of the Renaissance Man, he rejected the warning of "he who encompasses too much, grasps too little" from a young age. Specialization always ended up boring him. This led him down various paths of humanistic-scientific exploration and search. He lived the first half of his life in Uruguay and the second in the United States, where he currently resides. After 27 years away from his homeland, he has set out to tell stories of the Montevideo of his grandparents, of his upbringing under the strong influence of Italian traditions and idiosyncrasies on his father's side. "I wrote little with a pencil when I was young. However, I was always jotting down memories in my mind with the intention of telling them someday. Well, that moment has arrived."

Made in the USA
Columbia, SC
03 August 2024

39641166R00186